HOW THE DUKE STOLE CHRISTMAS

A STOLEN KISSES NOVELLA

ALANNA LUCAS

ISBN: 978-0-9985314-6-5

Sebastiani Press

P.O. Box 1234

Simi Valley, Ca 93062

Cover by Dar Albert

❀ Created with Vellum

For my Family

CHAPTER 1

October 1819

Leaning against the cool fluted column near the rear of the ballroom, Greystone viewed the spectacle before him. Fancy peacocks, draped figures with dark masks, and fairytale nymphs all seemed to be searching for mischievous adventure. And yet, even with all the whimsey, everywhere he turned it seemed as if the gossipmongers were staring only at him. Despite the dark cloak and grey mask he wore, he suspected they knew exactly who he was.

"Glowering is not going to make the evening progress any faster." A faint whisper of jasmine tickled his nostrils. *Mother.*

She was the only reason he endured this madness. She had been pestering him for years to join her for the Season or one of these house parties, but each time, he had managed to create some excuse. However, on his last visit to Castle Greystone, in a moment of weakness he'd promised to attend one function this year. Since the year was almost at an end, this was the one he'd chosen, where he'd assumed no one would suspect his identity, and would leave him mostly alone. He'd been wrong. The moment he'd walked into the opulent ballroom, he'd been cornered first by Lady Capers, then Lady Neville. His mood was souring with each breath he took.

"I am not glowering. Perhaps I am surveying my surroundings, deciding on which masked lady I should ask to dance." He leaned toward his mother, attempting to add humor to his words. "Will she be the peacock? Or the enticing Grecian goddess? Or perhaps I should consider..." He glanced about the room, his gaze settling on a colorful concoction. "I don't even know how to describe that creature." A dreadful shudder rippled down his spine at the array of feathers and multi-colored ribbons exploding from the young lady's headdress.

Mother turned her gaze in the direction of where Greystone was looking. She opened her fan with a gentle flick of her elegant gloved hand and brought it up close to her lips. "Oh dear, that is an unfortunate display," she whispered out on a sly giggle.

A loud, involuntary sigh escaped Greystone's lips.

As if reading his thoughts, she turned her attention back to her son. Her eyes peered through her green and gold mask, pleading with concern as she spoke. "If you would just make some sort of attempt to be social it would—"

Focusing again on the display of masks parading through the space, he retorted, "I've been social, just not in public."

"Really, Theodore, do you have to be so…so vulgar? I'm merely worried about you. I just thought—"

Cutting off her lecture, he let out a heavy sigh. He knew exactly what she was trying to do. "Mother, I am here this evening. Please, just be satisfied with that victory."

No matter how hard he tried, betrayal haunted him, followed him. Six years ago, he'd had everything within his grasp; a beautiful fiancée, an impressive title, and a brother who was his best friend. And now, all he was left with was a grand title and an empty scarred heart, with an impregnable wall around it. Why was he even here?

Even behind her mask, he could see her jaw tighten. "Please make an effort this evening. For my sake."

Guilt soured in his stomach. What was he going to do with her?

He met her gaze. Sadness and heartache weighed down her lovely green eyes. There had been too many losses in recent years. *Damn his brother*.

She placed a soft hand on his arm. "Please." The pleading look in her eyes nearly broke his heart.

With great reluctance, he responded, "For you, Mother, I will make an excellent display." Her eyes brightened. *For one evening, I will make you happy*. One evening was all he was capable of giving. "Now, if you will excuse me, I must find a suitable dance partner."

But before he could make an escape, she raised a gloved hand to cheek. "I just want you to find happiness, Theodore." And with that final comment, she walked away leaving him to ponder what *exactly* would make him happy. Every time he thought he'd found some semblance of happiness, the bitter taste of betrayal reared its ugly head and plunged him further into the depths of guilt and remorse. Why, after all these years, would anything be any different?

A ruckus careened from across the room as a group of boisterous young gents set on mischief cackled as they drew every eye in attendance to them. Greystone had tilted his head to see what had caused them to act in such a manner when he spied a quartet of masked ladies entering the ballroom with all the joy and exuberance of youth.

Envy heated his veins. What would it be like to be young

and carefree again? To be able to turn back the clock and set things to rights.

Past the quartet of colorful masks, a lone lady trailed. She glanced about the ballroom as if she were looking for someone when her eyes settled on him. For one brief moment their eyes locked before she quickly lowered her lashes. He was certain that underneath the blue mask edged with gold, a deep blush tainted her creamy skin.

Out of the corner of his eye, he noticed his mother glancing toward the lady, then offering an encouraging nod his way. Mother was relentless in her quest this evening, he'd give her that much.

"The Duchess of Greystone giving you trouble this evening?" He heard the teasing tone of his best friend, Lord Kinsley, over his shoulder.

"As you well know, she would like to see me married, settled—preferably with a baby on the way—all by the end of the year." This had become the standard topic of conversation between the two friends of late. Both had meddling mothers who seemed to have nothing better to do than to pester their only sons.

"*Tsk, Tsk.* That doesn't leave much time." Kinsley said with a hint of teasing sarcasm. "Life does not seem to be fair for two kindhearted gentlemen such as ourselves."

"Kindhearted indeed." Greystone was never one to express his woes out loud. His wounds ran deep, and the wall he'd built around his heart was tall. He would not fall victim to anyone. Better to appear cold-hearted than to endure heartbreak…again.

"Are you going to the north for the festive season?"

He had no intention of returning to Castle Greystone any time soon. "Just as soon as my obligations here are met." He continued to admire the group of young ladies. He nodded in the direction of the lady clad in light blue. No, not quite blue, but some heavenly variation of the color that glimmered in the candlelight. “Do you know who she is?”

Her elaborate mask covered the upper half of her face, but thankfully did not conceal her delicate plump lips. Her movements were graceful yet sweet all at the same time. She appeared genuinely enthralled with the activity around her, which was a welcome change to the normal husband-hunting antics that usually were par for the course at such events.

Greystone continued to admire her. She was beautifully refreshing amongst the types one found parading around at these functions.

Kinsley’s gaze followed to where he was nodding. “I haven’t a clue, but I would like to discover—”

Without tearing his gaze from the young woman who had caught his attention, Greystone raised his hand to stop Kinsley. “I saw her first.” He couldn’t take his eyes off her. There was something about her that he found intriguing.

“And I suppose a duke trumps a viscount?”

“In this case, yes.”

Without further word, Greystone took his leave, passing curious onlookers as he headed straight for the lovely lady in the tantalizing mask.

He should have gone to the master of ceremonies and acquired a proper introduction, but he was a duke, and besides, it was a ridiculous rule in his estimation. Not to mention this was a masquerade and Lady Trumble, their hostess, had a ridiculous notion about everyone knowing everyone regardless of masks, although few had obliged.

All he wanted was a dance, one enjoyable dance, to fulfill his promise to his mother. As pleasurable as it would be, he was not going to whisk the young woman off to some dark alcove or seduce her in the garden. He reminded himself that she was a proper lady of the *ton*, not a candidate for the position of his next mistress. And besides, the wall he'd built around his heart would not allow for such frivolities with a proper lady.

Later, in the still of night, he knew he would question his sanity. He should have chosen a partner who did not entice him from the first moment he'd set eyes on her. He always guarded his feelings with extreme caution. However, he *had* promised his mother that he would indulge in one dance. He might disobey his mother's wishes from time to time, but once he made a promise, he never broke it.

The crush of people continued to part and let him pass, as hushed whispers about his possible identity coursed through the room.

He paid no heed but stayed the course. Only once he reached the masked lady did he relax. "May I have the honor of the next dance?"

Crystal clear blue eyes gleamed in the candlelight. "I would be honored." Her long dark brown eyelashes fluttered and then lowered as if in embarrassment.

Casual conversation had never been a strong suit for Greystone. Get straight to the point had always been his motto. But suddenly he had a strong desire to know more about her. Perhaps it was just a trick of his imagination, or that he'd been a hermit for far too long, but it was as if there was some invisible connection pulling him toward her.

"Thank you for accepting my hand." He offered it as he guided her to toward the dance floor and waited for the remaining couples to assemble.

As she worried her bottom lip, he wondered if it tasted as

good as it looked. *Oh hell.* He needed to rein in his thoughts. What was it about her?

"I suppose I should have declined your offer to dance, especially since it is a waltz and we have not been properly introduced." The sweet, teasing tone of her voice further tugged at his heartstrings.

"It is a ridiculous rule."

Her blue eyes softened behind the mask as she smiled. "I agree. And it is a masked ball after all."

Despite his desire for anonymity, he was curious about his dancing partner. "And whom do I have the pleasure of dancing with?"

"You're not supposed to inquire; that takes the mystique out of the evening," she replied lightly.

"I assure you, the evening will not lose its allure if I know your name." He was enjoying the playful banter, and for a moment, he could almost forget the past. Almost.

She seemed to think about it for a moment. "Miss Leybourne," she whispered out in a far too enticing tone. Did she have any idea how her spirited nature affected him? *Damn*, it had been far too long since he'd had a woman warming his bed.

The first soft chords of the waltz resonated through the ballroom. He took her hand in his, then settled his other on her back. Although the top of Miss Leybourne's head barely reached his shoulder, they seemed to fit perfectly together.

Don't be fooled. The warning echoed in his head.

"Is anything the matter?" Her caring blue gaze edged past some of the betrayal that his heart clung to. *How was she penetrating the wall around his heart?*

"It has been quite a few years since I danced." That wasn't entirely a lie, but he could not, would not tell her the truth. Not wanting to hurt her feelings, he added, "And even more since I danced with such a charming lady."

Miss Leybourne offered a half-smile that implied she did not quite believe him. He returned it with one of his own. The dance slowed, and as he continued to hold her in his arms, he realized he was falling under her spell. For the first time in years, he'd enjoyed a dance.

How was that even possible after one turn on the dance-floor? How was that possible after what he'd endured? Miss Leybourne was a dangerous creature indeed. Love was a far-fetched luxury for a select few, and love at first sight simply did not exist.

All too soon, it was time for him to return Miss Leybourne to her party.

"I bid you a good evening, Miss Leybourne. I hope to make your acquaintance again." He took his leave wondering what the hell had gotten into him. Not only had he enjoyed a dance with a proper lady of the *ton*, he had opened a Pandora's Box hoping to steal a moment with her later. The uneasiness in his gut told him it would not be a good idea.

No sooner had he left Miss Leybourne's side than Lady Blanch crossed the room with eagerness and much enthusiasm. The woman was abominable in every sense of the word.

"Your Grace," she called to him as if he were a close friend. "I thought it was you. I spied Her Grace speaking with you earlier and was convinced that it was you." She waved her hand. "And it is!"

Barely keeping his annoyance in check, he muttered, "Good evening, Lady Blanch."

Proper manners had been instilled in him since birth, but he was having a difficult time remembering why.

"Lady Capers and I were just discussing your very rare appearance this evening and hoped it means that you are re-entering society." The woman blathered on and on, about exactly what Greystone was unsure.

It was past time that he should take his leave. He had fulfilled his obligation to his mother. He was just about to make his excuses when Lady Blanch wagged a chubby finger at him. "A man of your position needs an heir, and as luck would have it, my daughter—"

"Madam," he ground out between his teeth, "I have no intentions of being caught in the parson's noose."

"B…but the dukedom?" Disbelief laced each syllable.

"Is my concern. Good evening."

He stormed toward the entrance hall, not caring who he disturbed. The nerve of that woman. What gave her the right to discuss such a personal topic? In just a few minutes he would be free of this nonsense. Free to search for more pleasurable entertainments.

With each stride, sounds of the gathering died to a gentle murmur, and his thoughts edged to the forefront of his mind. A heavy sigh coursed through his body, halting his progress.

However much he detested women such as Lady Blanch, her words had struck a chord with him that he simply could not ignore. Truth be told, he'd been thinking about the dukedom a lot of late. It was his duty at as the seventh Duke of Greystone to marry, beget an heir, and provide stability for generations to come.

He changed direction, deciding it might be in his better interest to return to the ballroom. There, he spied Miss Leybourne, tucked behind one of the large marble statues that lined the long white gallery.

Some unseen force pulled him toward her, as a glimmer of hope crept its way into his weary soul. Moonlight from one of the many floor-to-ceiling windows shimmered against the silvery blue of her mask, caressing her features.

"We meet again, Miss Leybourne."

As she shifted her gaze from the moonlit landscape to his, the smile in her eyes contained a sensuous flame. "So we do."

The need she stirred was almost dizzying as he closed the distance. Best to stamp those desires down. Casual conversation would better suit. "Are you enjoying the evening?"

Her brows drew together, pondering his question. "I… suppose, yes."

"You don't sound certain." Miss Leybourne was young and vibrant. How could she not enjoy diversions such as these?

A slight giggle escaped her lips. "No, I suppose I'm not." She worried her bottom lip again. "I guess I've grown rather tired of large balls and crowded entertainments."

He offered his arm. "Perhaps a stroll along the marble gallery would help with what ails you?"

Without hesitation she took his arm. They walked in serene silence down the gallery further away from prying eyes for several minutes before Miss Leybourne questioned, "Are you going to reveal your identity?"

With this alluring creature at his side, Greystone was in no rush to end the mystique of the evening. Ignoring her question, he took her gloved hand in his, slid his other hand to the small of her back, and began waltzing. Moonlight swirled around, enveloping them in a timeless moment that existed only for them.

Something intense coursed between them, and without thought for consequence, he lowered his head and took her mouth in a gentle kiss that sang through his veins, bringing him back to life.

His first kiss since the betrayal. He hadn't tasted a woman's lips in six years. The act was far too intimate. But here he was, kissing this woman as if his life depended on it.

In the quiet of his rooms later, he would question his sanity. He'd bedded his fair share of women since the betrayal but had insisted on no kissing. What was it about her that he could not resist? Was it duty that dictated the survival of the dukedom, or something deeper?

Reality fought its way through the moonlit haze of desire. He rested his forehead against hers. "You should return before someone notices." Lovely blue eyes searched his, the unspoken question lingering on her lips. "I will join you for the unmasking."

Her smile touched every inch of his body. "I'm enjoying the evening much more, thank you."

"It has been my pleasure," he said before brushing another soft kiss across her lips.

He watched as she retraced her steps toward the ballroom. Hope continued to surge through his body. Perhaps he could lay the past to rest.

Ten minutes later, he decided enough time had passed to rejoin the throng. He did not want to sully Miss Leybourne's name with unwarranted gossip. Heaven knew the gossipmongers did not need much to create a stir. He was just on the perimeter of the great hall when the sound of giggles broke his progress.

"I think he will be mine within a fortnight." A young woman's voice echoed softly from a dark room. The voice sounded vaguely familiar. He halted just beyond the open door and leaned in to listen more closely.

"Do you really believe that you can seduce him?"

"I have no doubt," the lady said with a confidence that churned his stomach. But nothing could have prepared him for the words that followed. "I am a Leybourne, after all."

So that was Miss Leybourne's intention this evening. She was interested in snaring a duke? The surreal moment they'd shared soured in his gut. Well, she would have to look someplace else. This duke would not fall such antics.

He might have been fooled by her this evening, but never again. He would not, not now. He would not, not ever. Not here in London. Not anywhere.

Never again.

CHAPTER 2

December 1819

Sequestered in a carriage, trudging along muddy roads was not how she thought she would be spending the festive season. Patience was losing, well…her patience. The journey had started pleasantly enough but quickly turned into one fraught with one problem after another. In all honestly, she was quite surprised her aunt wanted to travel at this time of year. She supposed the timely invitation from Aunt Agnes's dearest friend to spend Christmas with her at Castle Greystone at least meant a reprieve from all the gossip.

The gossipmongers had been quite ruthless in their speculation as to why Patrick had not attended their younger sister Parnell's wedding earlier this month, never mind that his wife was due to deliver a baby at any moment. Not to mention that, being a Leybourne, of course there were rumors about how Parnell had seduced and snared the Duke of Bedford. Patience knew better. Both her siblings had married for love, and so would she. But, as of late, she had begun to wonder if she would ever find that special someone. She wanted a love like her parents had, except without all the tragedy.

She inwardly sighed as her stomach turned and knotted. This was to be her first Christmas without her siblings. Family meant everything to her, and now… the heavy ache of more change weighed down on her.

"Are you alright, dearie?"

"I suppose."

Aunt Agnes raised a delicate grey brow as if not quite believing her before returning to her needlepoint.

"I'm just tired of being trapped in this carriage." Patience decided to broach another topic that had been on her mind since they'd received the Christmastide invitation from the Dowager Duchess of Greystone. "I still don't understand why His Grace would not want to spend time with his mother?"

Didn't he know how precious one's parents were? How it all could change in the blink of an eye? Painful memories of her mother's, and then father's, funerals flashed before her eyes. She could feel the anxiety rise with each breath she took. She swallowed hard, begging the memoires to stay down. It was always worse at this time of year. She never talked about those feelings, and she wished to keep it that way.

Not looking up from her mistletoe needlepoint, Aunt Agnes responded without elaboration, "Castle Greystone holds unpleasant memories for His Grace."

Patience was thankful the elusive Duke of Greystone would not be in attendance this time. He had rarely been seen in polite society, but rumors had swirled about him for years. She wondered if any of them were true. She supposed the part about him running his brother off the estate, wielding a sword, was utter nonsense. But there were so many other tales of mistresses and even one about a fiancée. Despite her aunt's friendship with the Dowager Duchess, Patience had never met the Duke and hoped to keep it that way.

Pushing the carriage curtain aside, she peered out of the window at the passing countryside. The rain had stopped, and vast patches of blue filled the sky. She lost herself in private thoughts as the dusk sky slowly darkened. Soon, dozens of stars would begin to twinkle. Ever since she was little, twinkling stars had always reminded her of chandeliers in a ballroom. But since Lady Trumble's ball, they'd reminded her of a perfect dance and a handsome gentleman clad in black with a dark grey mask. His green eyes reminded her of mistletoe leaves. And his kiss...*ah, his kiss*. The memory of it still sent a delicious shiver down her spine.

Clearly, her feelings were one-sided, which made the sting all that much more hurtful. He'd said he would come to her at the unmasking, but he disappeared. Over the past couple of months, it had become easier to try to convince her heart that she'd conjured up the entire scene, but even she didn't believe her imagination was *that* good.

She inhaled deeply.

"Are you certain you're not taking ill, dearie?"

"No, just tired of being cooped up in the carriage." It wasn't a lie, but it wasn't entirely the truth. Her masked gentleman was the current cause of her angst. *He's not yours, nor is he a gentleman*, she reminded herself, hoping to ease the ache in her heart.

With a quick glance out the window, Aunt Agnes responded with confidence. "We should be nearing Castle Greystone soon."

Wanting to avoid further questioning, she turned her attention back to the changing landscape. She hoped the castle would come into view before it got too dark. She had never ventured to this far north before and was fascinated by all that she saw. The vast rolling hills and the abundance of wildlife were all food for her starving imagination.

In the far distance, the castle loomed on the horizon, illuminated by the setting sun behind it. Two large turrets reached up toward the sky. *Imagine the views from up there.* The walls stood tall and foreboding. A soft giggle escaped her lips.

"What's so amusing?"

"I was just imagining what dark secrets lurk within the castle walls."

Aunt Agnes's wide grin teased from across the seat. "You have quite the imagination, Patience. Perhaps you should spend a little less time reading and more time contemplating your future. I'm not going to be around forever, dearest. One day you will have to marry. The life of a spinster would not suit you."

That was a sobering thought.

"My imagination makes life interesting." Patience could not tell her aunt the truth. Her imagination was what had helped her survive the darkest times of life. First, her mother's illness and death, and then her father's quick descent into debauchery that had led to his ultimate demise. It was during those dark moments that Patience and Parnell would make up fairytales. She missed her sister. Parnell had always been part of her life. They were practically twins, a year apart to the day. And now, Parnell was married. Tears stung her eyes.

So lost in her thoughts, Patience had not realized that they had turned down the drive and were approaching the front entrance until her aunt whispered, "Castle Greystone."

They passed through a magnificent stone gate connected to a stone rampart and then passed a gatekeeper's cottage, which stood as sentinel. It looked like a miniature version of the castle she had spied in the distance just a short time ago. Streaks of waning sunlight cascaded across the land, bringing mystical creatures to life.

It must have been wonderful to grow up amongst such fascination. One would never want to leave such a magical place. She hoped the weather would cooperate, and she would have time to explore the beautiful countryside over the coming fortnight.

After what felt like hours later, they finally arrived at the entrance to the castle. Dark clouds had blanketed the land now, almost extinguishing the moonlight.

The moment the carriage stopped, efficient, liveried footmen clad in green and white readied the steps. A fresh, cool wind whipped through the carriage as the door opened. Aunt Agnes coughed slightly before she pulled her cloak about her frail shoulders and accepted assistance. Patience held her breath as she watched her aunt's unsteady descent. The journey had taken its toll on her relative. A couple of days rest on solid ground and hopefully the older woman would be back to normal.

The sight of Castle Greystone took her breath away. Stonework stretched up toward the black sky. It must be a hundred feet high. She had seen impressive homes before, but none that had compared to this.

They were quickly ushered into the entry hall where they were greeted by the Dowager Duchess.

"At long last. I feared something ill might have happened." Her Grace embraced Aunt Agnes, and then turned her attention to Patience. "I am so pleased you were able to accompany your aunt, Miss Leybourne."

"Thank you, Your Grace." It had been a couple of months since she had last seen the Dowager Duchess at Lady Trumble's ball, but she seemed to have aged in those months. Worry and sadness creased the delicate skin around her eyes.

"You must be tired from your journey. After you settle, we will dine." Her Grace's tone was warm and welcoming.

Patience followed behind at a snail's pace. If she was in awe of the outside of Castle Greystone, no words known could describe the impressive interior with its high ceilings, exquisite artwork, and colorful tapestries. It was grand and filled with wondrous treasures, but it was more than that; despite all the grandeur, it felt like a home.

After getting settled and changing out of their traveling clothes, Patience and Aunt Agnes were shown to the dining room.

"We need not stand on ceremony," Her Grace said as they entered yet another opulent room decorated in deep green and gold. "Dinner will be informal this evening."

Even the food smelled more extravagant in the country.

Too enthralled with the duck and mushroom sauce, Patience was not able to say two words during the second course. By the time dessert arrived, she was certain that Her Grace must think her mute.

"And what traditions do you enjoy during Christmastide, Miss Leybourne?"

Before her siblings had gone off and married? She inwardly sighed.

"Spending time with my family."

"I would have to agree."

The sadness in the Dowager's voice nearly broke Patience's heart and before she could stop herself the words started pouring out. "I cannot fathom why your son does not see it as essential that he should spend time with you during the Yuletide." Aunt Agnes gave Patience an astonished glare and looked as if she were about to deliver a scolding. Heat inflamed Patience's cheeks. Before the situation worsened, she corrected herself. "I apologize, Your Grace. I should not have been so carefree with my words. Sometimes I say things before I think if they are proper or not."

Her Grace's warm smile eased her embarrassment a little. "You do not need to apologize. You are quite right." She let out a long, almost painful sigh. "Ever since my younger son ran off, Greystone has not been the same. Arthur has been dead four years and things still have not improved."

Patience did not want to press the topic any more than she had already. As it was, she knew she would be receiving a lecture from her aunt about proper etiquette, especially in the presence of the Dowager Duchess. Somehow, she managed to keep her thoughts to herself through the rest of the dessert course. She owed that monumental feat to the sugared almonds. Never in her life had she tasted anything so decadent.

The evening greatly improved when Her Grace offered to take Patience and Aunt Agnes on a little tour of the house, informing them that, on the morrow, she would show them the sculpture gallery.

Patience fell behind, admiring a beautiful tapestry that encompassed an entire wall, edge to edge and floor to ceiling. Even in the candlelight, it was magnificent. She leaned to take a closer look at the intricate details.

A blue and gold intertwined rope framed the magnificent tapestry. In the foreground, an elegantly dressed lady sat perched atop a white horse. Several playful dogs pranced in the lush surrounding vegetation. In the distance, set against the rolling green countryside, was a castle quite similar to Castle Greystone, or at least some medieval version of it.

"It is one of my favorite pieces in the house," the Dowager Duchess's sweet voice said over Patience's shoulder.

"It is breathtaking." Patience fought every urge not to reach out and touch the beautiful horse.

"When I was first brought here as a bride, my husband

would tease me, saying that I spent more time admiring that tapestry than I did him."

A giggle escaped Patience's lips. "I would've been accused of the same. You have such a wonderful collection, I can imagine it would be difficult not to get distracted while seeing to your duties."

"I remember my first visit to the castle." Aunt Agnes's eyes sparkled with a youthful mischievousness of years gone by. "The hedge maze was what kept me in awe. On more than one occasion, Clarice and I got quite lost in that maze."

"You have a hedge maze?" Patience's excitement echoed off the walls. She'd only ever read about them, but would very much enjoying exploring one, setting her imagination free.

"If weather permits, we can take a turn in the grounds tomorrow."

"That's very kind of you, Your Grace." Patience was not expecting to be entertained by the Dowager Duchess during her stay. Her only purpose in coming to Castle Greystone was to be near her aunt during the Christmas season.

"Do you…" Aunt Agnes's words trailed off as she succumbed to a series of little coughs.

"Are you unwell, Aunt Agnes?" Patience rushed to her relative's side and placed her hand on the older woman's forehead. "You feel quite warm."

Aunt Agnes pulled a delicate white handkerchief from her sleeve and dabbed her face. "I feel quite tired, but then again I suppose I'm not used to traveling."

That was exactly how it had begun with Mother. For days she'd complained about fatigue and then…

Panic coursed through Patience's veins. "We should send for a doctor or—"

Her Grace began to step away, speaking over her shoulder. "I'll have Boris go for—"

"No," her aunt waved her hand. "I'm just a little tired, nothing more." She offered a smile that Patience assumed was supposed to put her at ease. "Nothing that a night of rest won't cure."

"But…if you are unwell, it could be more than just fatigue."

"Agnes," Her Grace began in an informal, yet firm tone, "Please, it's no trouble at all."

"Listen to the two of you fussing over me. I am not on my deathbed, just tired after the lengthy journey."

"Very well, we will let you rest." Patience bent and kissed Aunt Agnes's forehead. The spicy scent of carnation filled her nostrils as tears threatened to spill.

"You have to promise me that the moment you feel any worse, you will allow me to send for a doctor," Her Grace insisted.

Aunt Agnes offered a sweet smile. "I promise. Now, I think it past time for me to retire."

CHAPTER 3

After checking on her still-sleeping aunt in the morning, Patience joined Her Grace for a tour of the hedge maze. But no sooner had they ventured outside than the rain descended on them in heavy sheets and they were forced to retreat. Her Grace altered their plans, giving Patience a thorough tour of the house, sharing stories, showing hidden treasures and secret passageways. They spent a most enjoyable three hours in each other's company.

They entered what once was the Great Hall in the medieval part of the castle, but now looked like a wing at the new British Museum. Pride filled Her Grace's voice, "This is my favorite room of the house."

Crisp white marble statues filled the half-dozen niches, several large, sparkling chandeliers hung from the white coffered ceiling, and huge, intricate tapestries filled the spaces between the tall white fluted columns. Elegantly upholstered settees were strategically placed to maximize one's viewing pleasure of the fine display of artwork and sculptures.

Patience could hardly wait. It was Christmas Eve; decorations would soon be hung and the Yule log lit. Her excitement spilled over into words. "This room will look splendid once it's decorated with greenery and red ribbon."

No sooner had the words left Patience's mouth than the Dowager Duchess's face sagged with sadness, her eyes brimming with unshed tears.

"I…I'm sorry. I shouldn't have presumed…What I meant to say…." Patience knew she sounded like a simpleton, but she could not seem to form the words for a suitable apology. She really did need to control her thoughts and speech.

"You have nothing to apologize for." Shaking her head, grief marred the Dowager's features. "It has been years since this house has had the joy of being decorated for Christmastide. Not since…" Her Grace inhaled deeply before clearing her throat. "And besides, my son—"

After scolding Patience for her inappropriate comment during dinner last night, Aunt Agnes had shared just a little of Her Grace's life, and why sadness always seemed to be lingering in her eyes. She'd had a fairytale wedding, married a man she'd adored, and who'd adored her even more in return. Two sons had completed their family, but jealousy and a fallacious acceptance of a betrothal changed everything.

Patience could not imagine being jealous of either of her siblings, nor could she imagine how anyone could purposefully deceive another.

Long silent seconds passed, and she wondered if she should apologize again.

A moment later, Her Grace's eyes brightened, and a wide smile softened her features. "Would you do me the honor of overseeing the decorating?"

Patience opened and closed her mouth several times, too shocked by the request to do anything more. Her Grace raised a questioning brow waiting for her answer. "It…it wouldn't be proper for me—I mean this is your home, and you're a Duchess."

Her Grace laughed at Patience's statement. "I wasn't always a Duchess. And besides, this *is* my home and I would be most pleased it you would do me this favor. I am not getting any younger and I would most enjoy having the house look festive for once."

Patience tried to come up with another reason why she should decline. It just didn't seem proper for her to assume such an important, and not to mention personal, role within the house. Her Grace gave her a sad sideways glance and Patience's heart lurched. What harm could there be in decorating Castle Greystone? It's not as if the Duke was going to grace them with his presence, and even if he did, she wanted to do this for Her Grace.

With her mind made up, she said, "I promise I will make your home festive beyond your wildest imaginings."

Joy bubbled in Her Grace's voice. "That is quite a promise. I should warn you, I have a grand imagination." She clasped her hands together. "Now, what do we need to get started?"

For the next several hours Patience organized servants and decorations.

Her Grace had given Patience permission to decorate the Great Hall, music room, both parlors, and the entry hall, along with an army of servants at her disposal to achieve the task. She wanted everything to be perfect. This would be a Christmas to remember!

She directed several servants assigned to help her with the mantle decorations. "Please, bring the greenery and ivy to the table and we'll begin on the festoons."

She was thankful for the assistance; she could not achieve such a monumental task on her own. When she was a young girl, her family would spend the entire evening decorating their house together. She tightly wound a white ribbon around a spicy bundle of evergreens reflecting on bygone Christmases with her parents and Patrick and Parnell. After her mother passed away, the spirit of the season had died with her. Patience longed to bring that joy back.

She'd thought after her brother had married and their prospects improved, she would experience some of that joy, but it constantly seemed to evade her.

She dismissed those thoughts. There was much to be done and so little time.

The table was overflowing with red and white silk ribbons, ivy, holly, garlands, and other fragrant greenery. She meticulously created bows to adorn the fireplaces and assembled decorative boughs.

She braided long pieces of ivy and silky red ribbon together, just the way her mother had shown her when she was a little girl. She'd always wanted to be more like her mother, who had been kind and gentle, and with not an ounce of temper. Time and time again, Patience had proved her own temper got the better of her more often than she wanted to acknowledge.

With great care, she weaved the decorative garland that would go across the mantle. She took two steps back and admired her work. This *would* be a lovely Christmas. The spirit of the season was slowly creeping its way into her soul. She had been feeling more alive here in the past few hours than she had in years. She wouldn't think about the future, she would just enjoy the moment.

"The house looks lovely." The sound of Her Grace's voice brought her out of her musings. There would be plenty of quiet hours in the still of night to contemplate her emotions. “I can’t remember when it looked so wonderfully festive.”

“Thank you, Your Grace. All that’s left is to bring in the Yule log.”

“*Your Grace* is much too formal. In my home, please call me Clarice. We’ve spent a lovely day together, you’ve decorated my home, and we’ve become friends. We need not stand on ceremony.”

“Oh, I couldn’t. You’re a Duchess and I simply couldn’t. It simply would not be proper.”

“I have a lovely name that I rarely get to hear anymore.” Her Grace leaned in and gave Patience a little wink. “One of the downsides to being a Duchess.”

Patience began to protest again, but her words fell on deaf ears. “But…I…”

Her Grace took Patience’s hand in hers and squeezed with more strength than she thought a woman of her age possessed. “I usually get my way,” she said with a teasing smile. “And besides, I wasn’t always a Duchess. I was born the daughter of a baron. Please. It would give me great pleasure if you would.”

Patience knew some members of the *ton* did not stand on such formal protocol, but she was rather surprised that a Duchess would think this way. In the end, she did not believe this was an argument she would win. “I would be honored.”

“Now that’s all settled, let’s have the men bring in the Yule log.”

~

CASTLE GREYSTONE ROSE PROUDLY from a bluff, the rough countryside at its back mocking Greystone as he neared the house, memories flooding his mind; painful memories that had not died with the ones that had betrayed him.

The walls around his heart, around his soul, stood firm. He would not let anyone penetrate those walls, especially after what occurred at Lady Trumble's ball two months prior. For one brief moment, he'd believed he could let his guard down, that he could find happiness again. One waltz with a blue-eyed beauty had tempted him in a way he'd never thought possible.

Not just a waltz. That moonlit kiss had been his undoing, but then…

He had been festering for months over what had happened that evening. Between the gossip and whispers—and Miss Leybourne's deceitfulness—he had found no peace. More than anything, he regretted arguing with his mother that very night. In the heat of the moment he'd spewed awful lies.

"Mother, do whatever suits you. I just don't care. I will not be returning to Castle Greystone. Not for Great Aunt June's eightieth birthday celebration. Not even for Christmas-tide." His spiteful words echoed in his ears as they ate away at him, one syllable at a time.

Truth be told, he did care. That's why he had to return home, to prove to her—and himself—that he *could* care. He knew she was just as hurt as he was, but he didn't know how to make it better. It had always been simpler to keep his feelings buried deep and keep his distance.

The wind whipped at his back, pushing him home as the rain pelted his face, jeering at his poor decision to embark on this journey on such a miserable day. But he had left himself no choice with all the procrastinating he'd done over the past week as to whether he should or should not come.

Karl's hooves sank in the slushy mud slowing their pace. He rubbed his mount's saturated neck, urging him on. They would be at Castle Greystone within the hour and he would ensure the horse was well-rewarded.

He'd just entered the stable yard when he was met by one of the stable lads. "Your Grace, we were not expecting…" His words came in short apologetic spurts.

Greystone dismounted, tossed the reins to the groom, and stormed off to the house. The terrible weather and delayed arrival had put him in a foul mood. It was better for him not to speak rather than lash out. Since the hour was late, he would not disturb his mother tonight. Besides, after a hot bath and a good night's sleep, he would be better company.

The force of the wind pushed the door wide, revealing his rather shocked butler. "Your Grace," Boris said, trying to contain his surprise.

The moment he went into the entry hall he knew something was amiss, and it wasn't just that he detested this house and all the memories within it that continued to taunt him. He inhaled deeply and was met with the crisp scent of evergreen. He detested Christmastide. He detested the whole damn season. He stormed in the direction of the odor, with Boris on his heels.

"We were not expecting…and Her Grace…"

Greystone waved his hand to silence the butler. "Who did this?" He growled as he entered the Great Hall. He knew very well his mother would not go against his wishes and have the house decorated, not after all these years.

Dread sank into his gut.

Was she ill? That would be the only reason she would defy his wishes.

He did not wait for Boris to respond. "I want it all taken down tonight. I do not want even a trace of mistletoe left behind." His growl rumbled through the hall. He reached up and tore down a long garland. "All of it."

"Yes, Your Grace."

Greystone glared about the room. Every strand of ivy, every ribbon, every decoration goaded him, reminding him of all that he had lost.

His eyes focused on a shimmering red ribbon perfectly tied around a garland draped across the large mantle. The image of a blonde-haired beauty with charcoal eyes flashed through his mind. A warm summer's day, deep dimples, and a sweet smile still provoked him after all these years. He strolled to the mantle, grasped the red bow and ripped it down. Greenery, broken branches, and torn ribbon flitted to the floor. He did not want to remember.

He stormed to the side table, pulled the stopper from the decanter, and poured a healthy serving of brandy. He downed the amber liquid in one burning swallow that settled into the depths of his stomach. He just wanted everything to go away, decorations and all.

CHAPTER 4

Christmas morning

The moment sunlight filtered into her room, Patience wanted to run downstairs and see all the decorations in daylight. It took all her patience, which despite her name she did not possess in abundance, to wait until a decent hour to descend.

Everything had looked so splendid bathed in the glow of candlelight the previous evening, she was certain it would be even more wonderful in the full light of day. Just thinking of how all the greenery looked against the pure white marble in the Great Hall was enough to make her giddy.

After checking on her still sleeping aunt, she hurried toward the day parlor. She imagined the light filtering in, dancing against red and silver ribbons through the east facing windows, the sun warming the space on a cold winter's day, and the fresh scent of pine wafting.

Picking up her pace, she went toward the parlor. As she rounded the corner, she was met with…nothing.

She edged into the room, torn by conflicting emotions.

She blinked several times, hoping the sparse walls and empty mantle were just an awful trick of her imagination.

Where had all the decorations gone? Her heart sank and for a brief moment she thought she would cry. *What had happened? Had the Dowager Duchess of Greystone been robbed?*

That didn't make any sense. Why would someone steal ivy, holly, and ribbon, but leave valuable figurines and paintings? Confusion laced every thought that coursed through her mind. She stepped further into the room. All that remained was a small scrap of silver ribbon.

She'd bent down to pick it up when a fierce voice demanded, "Who the hell are you, and what are you doing here?"

She instantly came to attention, her hand practically holding her pounding heart in her chest. She clutched the silver ribbon as she turned around. She steeled her nerves, prepared to argue with the intruder, only to come face to face with…her masked gentleman.

It couldn't be him. What was *he* doing here?

Oh, no! Panic ruptured in her heart. She tried to find words—even one would suffice— but nothing. For the first time in her life, she was speechless.

Recognition flashed in his eyes before he growled out. "I shall ask only once more." The tall, imposing figure stepped closer.

She felt like a fox trapped by a hound. She was still trying to wrap her thoughts around the presence of this man, but before reason sank in, Clarice stormed into the undecorated room.

"What have you done, Theodore?"

Theodore? This was Her Grace's son? *This* brute was the

Duke of Greystone? Suddenly Patience felt lightheaded and entirely out of sorts. Worse, her feet were heavy as stone.

"*Good morning*, Mother," His Grace said in a restrained tone laced with more sarcasm than Patience believed she'd ever heard. Clearly, it was not going to be a good morning.

"What happened to all the decorations?" Clarice demanded.

"Will you not return the greeting?"

"Good morning, Theodore," Clarice offered, matching her son's sarcasm. "What have you done with my decorations?"

"I ordered them to be taken down." The Duke's tone was matter-of-fact, as if the removal of decorations *on* Christmas Day was a normal occurrence.

Patience stood and watched the episode unfold as if sitting in her brother's box at the theatre, watching *Othello*.

Clarice approached her son with a stern look on her face. She pointed one elegant finger at him as she ground out, "You cannot just walk in here and do whatever you want."

"This is my house and my decision. If I—"

"Theodore." Her Grace's firm tone sent a chill down Patience's spine. She did not want to witness what was certain to be a most ugly argument.

As the Dowager Duchess continued to scold the Duke, Patience backed out of the room one careful step at a time. Guilt settled in her stomach. She had overseen the decorating and now mother and son were at odds with one another because of her.

Only when Patience was safely away from the uncomfortable scene did she allow her mind to contemplate who the Duke of Greystone actually was.

She trudged through the halls in a daze. It *was* him.

What had she done to earn his wrath? Why had he disappeared before the unmasking? Surely, he remembered the kiss they'd shared? These and a thousand more questions swirled through her mind as reality stormed to the front of her thoughts. *He* was the elusive duke who rarely showed his face in polite society, and who was known for a trail of illustrious mistresses. Well, this was one woman who would not be fooled by him. Two could play at this game.

OUT OF THE corner of his eye, Greystone watched Miss Leybourne sneak out of the room like a common thief. He would not tolerate such behavior in his home. However, he couldn't deal with her until he'd set things to rights with his mother.

"Why is she here, Mother?"

"Since you had informed me that you would *not* be here for Christmas, I invited my dearest friend, Lady Leybourne, for a visit."

"I understand why Lady Leybourne is here, but why is *she* here?" He growled as he pointed toward the open door. "What could a beautiful…" he stopped mid-sentence.

Mother eyed him with curiosity. "Miss Leybourne is her niece." Then added salt to his wound. "I thought it would be a pleasant change to not be alone at the castle."

Greystone ran a frustrated hand through his hair. Mother was heaping on the guilt this morning. He did not want to be angry with her but was quickly losing his patience. Shifting his stance, he tried to control the urge to get the hell away, to leave this place. But he did not want to disappoint his mother. He would have to find another way to deal with Miss Leybourne.

"Why are you so angry?" Mother's voice was calm, almost eerie. A direct contrast to all the painful memories that being in this house brought forth.

"Why?" His voice rumbled through the white space. "Why do you insist on bringing up the past?"

Mother took a step closer, her gaze never leaving his. "I don't want to argue."

"What *do* you want?" Greystone said as he turned away from his mother's penetrating stare. Coming home had been a mistake.

"What any mother wants—for her children to be happy." A soft hand caressed his shoulder.

"I think it's too late for that, Mother."

"Only if you believe it is."

He was about to make some sarcastic retort when he turned and glanced down into his mother's sad eyes and changed his mind. He was at a loss for words. Anything he said would most likely hurt her, and he didn't want to be the reason—yet again—for her unhappiness.

Mother reached up and kissed his cheek. "It's good to have you home." She walked away, leaving him to contemplate her words. It *was* too late for him.

~

BOXING DAY

Apart from his brief tirade the previous morning, Patience had not seen or heard anything more of His Grace and preferred it that way. Although she thought it inappropriate, Greystone had not attended church, nor had he joined them for Christmas dinner. His foul mood and disturbing removal of all the decorations had darkened the spirit of the season. But just because she had not seen His Grace did not mean that he did not affect her.

If she stayed at Castle Greystone, she was bound to encounter *him* again. But no matter how much she wanted to immediately depart, she couldn't. Aunt Agnes was not well enough to travel, and one thing was for certain, she would not leave without her aunt. She would just have to wait till her relative was well enough and then they would return to London, where she could forget the Duke of Greystone forever.

With her mind made up, she went to inform Her Grace of her decision.

She found her in the recently-undecorated day parlor, surrounded by dozens of beautifully wrapped gifts. "You're just in time, Patience," Her Grace said with a bright smile.

"In time…for what, Your Grace?" She hesitated.

"To assist me with handing out the gifts to the servants," Her Grace began as if it were the most natural thing in the world for a guest to aid in this tradition. "And I thought the matter of my name was settled?" she teased.

Patience's mouth suddenly went dry. "Well…I thought since His Grace has arrived, it wouldn't be—"

"Never mind him," Clarice said with a wave of her hand before changing the subject. "Besides bringing in the Yule log, this is my favorite part of Christmastide."

"It simply wouldn't be proper."

"I will decide what's proper, not my son." It wasn't a scolding, but a firm statement.

Within moments, the staff began to assemble in the large space. Although Patience felt out of place, she was excited to participate in this tradition once again.

After Father had squandered all of their money and then killed himself, there had been no funds for gifts. There hadn't been any money for staff either. There simply had been nothing. A few of the most loyal and long-time servants stayed on. Her brother had tried everything to reverse their situation, but year after year it had only grown worse. It wasn't until he'd married Aveline that their situation improved.

Patience remembered the utter joy in the household the first Christmas after Patrick and Aveline married. The estate was prospering again, their finances were on the upturn, but most important, they were all together, healthy and happy.

Patience watched as the staff lined up in an orderly fashion to receive their boxes. The number of servants was quite impressive, and Clarice knew each one by name. It was quite clear she enjoyed this time-honored ritual.

As servants approached, Clarice handed them a neatly wrapped box and thanked them for their loyal service. They all beamed with her praise and well-wishes. It warmed Patience to her very core. If she were to ever have the privilege of dispersing gifts, she would want to be just like Her Grace, kind, generous, and sincere.

When the last servant had received their box, Clarice announced a special treat. There was to be dining, dancing, and much merriment, and everyone was invited.

After checking on her aunt and satisfied that her illness was not getting worse, Patience joined the festivities in the ballroom. She was enjoying the music and laughter, the general jollity of the season, but underneath the joy, a layer of hurtfulness was constricting her heart.

His Grace had fooled her.

He was not the dashing gentleman she had danced with at Lady Trumble's ball, and he was definitely not the same passionate man who had kissed her. His Grace was cold and distant, and extremely suspicious—of what she had no idea, and it was only the second day! Worse still, he was the only man who had ever stirred her senses. One kiss and she'd been smitten. It had far surpassed the couple of kisses previously bestowed. Just the thought made her… No, she mustn't think of His Grace or that kiss.

Hours later, the festivities were still energetic, but Patience needed a moment of quiet solitude. Her head had begun to throb with the constant worry that His Grace would storm into the room and halt the gaiety.

Slipping out the room, she removed her gloves as she strolled down the well-lit hall admiring the paintings along the way. Calm ensued as distant sounds of merriment faded into the recesses of the grand house. By the time she reached the Great Hall, the only sound that could be heard was her breathing.

Although none of the decorations had been displayed again—a topic Patience was not going to broach with Clarice—the Great Hall was still magnificent.

Dozens of candles illuminated the room, revealing the opulence of the Duke of Greystone's ancestral home. Richly detailed paintings and tapestries adorned the walls. Lavish artifacts and silver vases graced the tabletops. And not for the first time, Patience felt the castle, despite its grandness, was cozy and intimate. She suspected that it had something to do with only one of its current occupants. The Dowager Duchess of Greystone did not put on airs or throw her title about; she was genuine. In many ways, Clarice reminded Patience of her own mother. Perhaps that was why she was so drawn to the other woman.

"You seemed to have ensconced yourself within my household," a deep voice came from behind.

"Oh," she gasped, dropping her gloves as she turned around, her heart pounding wildly in her chest.

For the second time in so many days, His Grace had sneaked up on her. She wished she was still wearing her gloves. In a most unladylike fashion, she smoothed her damp palms down the front of her dress. Hopefully, he would not notice how nervous he was making her. Perhaps it was his tall figure, or the fact that he wore such dark colors, or the way his deep green eyes peered deep into her soul, or… *that perfect kiss*.

A far-too-pleasant shiver ran down her spine. She tried to shake off the all-too-many feelings that he stirred.

"Her…Her Grace invited me."

"Regardless, you appear to be taking an inventory." The Duke of Greystone's statement and tone was very off putting, and yet he eyed her like a man long deprived.

On several occasions she had overheard her brother and his friend joking about men being deprived. She assumed this was what they'd meant.

"I am doing no such thing," Her voice raised an octave, ricocheting off the walls. She waved her hand toward the gold-edged tapestry. "Why is it so wrong for someone to admire an object of beauty?"

"Nothing. Unless you are trying to land yourself a duke," he said under his breath as he walked away from her.

Oh, the man could be so infuriating!

"I don't care about titles," she yelled at him. He stopped in his tracks and stared at her. There was harshness in his eyes, but Patience could not control her words. "Despite what the *ton* believes, life is not about titles and soirées. It's about family and church and making memories. You have a wonderful mother and all you care about is avoiding her."

"That's not all I care about," he growled.

"Oh, that's right! You also care about avoiding social functions and being a duke."

"It is common knowledge amongst the *ton* that you and your family schemed for your brother to marry an heiress.

Now that's all settled, it's said that you have your eyes on a duke."

Unbelievable.

She stood tall, her head only reaching the top of his shoulder. Lifting her chin, she mustered a firm tone, "If you are implying that I am here to ensnare you in the parson's trap, then I regret to inform you that you are entirely incorrect. I do not intend to seduce you, trick you, or otherwise engage in *any* activities with you. In fact, I wish to forget our brief interlude at Lady Trumble's ball."

His Grace opened his mouth to speak, but she was not done. No, in fact, she had only just begun.

The words poured from her mouth in an uncontrollable deluge. "If you were not so preoccupied with your own selfishness, you might care to notice that you have a mother who loves you very much, and before you know it, she could be gone and then it will be too late. I don't care if you take my words to heart. I am not trying to steal from you. I am not trying to lure you with my femininity, hoping to secure a marriage proposal. Nor am I some deceitful light-skirt who wants the position of your mistress. And furthermore, I'm not some simpering, pampered miss who does not understand the ways of the world. I know what it's like to suffer, to…"

CHAPTER 5

I know what it's like suffer. The words lingered in the air before settling in the pit of Greystone's stomach.

"What do you mean?" He did not want to imagine Patience suffering. He wanted her dressed in beautiful clothes, reading her favorite book by the firelight, and warming his bed. *Oh, bloody hell.*

She didn't even acknowledge his question before she turned away and uttered under her breath, "Nothing." Her answer was short and curt, meant to push him away he supposed, but it had the opposite effect.

He grabbed her arm and swirled her around into the full circle of his arms to face him. He glanced down into her clear blue eyes. Sadness filled their cool depths. A thud struck his heart.

In that moment, he did not think she was trying to seduce him. In that moment, he saw her for more than a lady of the *ton* in want of a wealthy husband and title. In that moment, he saw someone who had been wounded. In that moment, the wall surrounding his heart began to shake and crumble just a little.

"Your Grace," Patience whispered out, never breaking eye contact.

He was at the crossroads. He wanted to kiss her again, to take away the sadness that pooled in her eyes, but he didn't know if he was strong enough to survive the torrent of emotions that she was beginning to stir in him.

He slowly lowered his head, wanting only a brief taste of what was surely forbidden fruit. Her intoxicating floral scent wrapped around him, pulling him closer. Her lips were so close…

Ahem. Boris cleared his throat, disrupting the moment.

Patience pulled away, a rush of pink staining her cheeks.

Greystone reluctantly looked away from her. "Yes?"

"Your Grace, Miss Clara Winslow and Mrs. Holloway are here to see you."

Winslow? Winslow was his family name. A distant cousin, perhaps? But he didn't know any Holloway. Dread and anxiety careened in his stomach before spreading rapidly throughout his body.

His silence prompted Boris to question, "Shall I show them to your study?"

"I will be there in a moment." He turned his attention back to Patience. "We will continue…our discussion later." He did not wait for a response, but walked away, toward his study and certain doom.

The uneasy feeling continued to toil within his gut. Nothing good was on the horizon. He should have stayed away. This place invited and festered with trouble. A soft gasp startled him out of his musings. He looked up to find an older woman and a little girl—no more than four or five years old— holding a small brown dog with large dark eyes, standing at the entrance to his study.

"Your Grace, I'm Mrs. Holloway," the old woman began with some trepidation in her voice. "I was Mrs. Winslow's maid until…" Her words trailed off. She cleared her throat before continuing. "Allow me to present Miss Clara Winslow, your brother's daughter."

Standing in the hall, where anyone might hear, was not good. He ushered them into the study.

Arthur had a daughter? Why hadn't he written or thought to return home? It was just like his brother to do something like this. Even in death, he somehow managed to create scandal and disrupt his life.

Greystone stood staring down at the little girl. She was the spitting image of Arthur, but in a delicate, feminine form. What did one even say to something this small?

The little girl's large green eyes—the same as his brother's, the same as his—filled with tears. Clara clutched the dog tighter as she scooted behind Mrs. Holloway, almost disappearing behind the large woman's serviceable grey skirt.

Greystone inhaled deeply and then slowly released his breath. "Good evening, Miss Clara." With his greeting she peered around Mrs. Holloway and eyed him. Now what would he say?

The dog began to squirm, its tail wagging with excitement. "This is Max," his niece whispered. *His niece.*

The words were still sinking in when his mother's voice rang out from down the hall. "Where is she?" The sound of rapid footsteps growing louder muddled his thoughts. How was he going to explain this?

"Oh, my!" Mother exclaimed as she rushed into the room toward Mrs. Holloway. She took one look at the little girl, bent down, and brought both the child and dog into a warm embrace. "She looks so much like him."

Explain what?

Years of sadness had been instantly erased from Mother's face. Even her tone seemed lighter. "I would guess that you're starving after such a long journey."

The little girl didn't answer but nodded her head with uncertainty.

"And I'm certain your dog would like a treat too?"

Clara's eyes lit up at the mention of her little dog. Mother had always had a way with children.

Hearing the word 'treat', the dog wiggled out of Clara's arms and rushed to where Greystone was standing and circled him twice before rushing back to Clara's side.

"Oh, yes, Max is most hungry."

"I know where Cook keeps all the best desserts." Mother held out her hand and the little girl quickly accepted it. It would have been a touching scene if Greystone had had a heart. The pair practically skipped out of the room with Max following close behind, hurrying toward the promise of sweets.

There would be no question as to what to do with the child. He had failed his mother, driven his brother off, and practically killed his father with his reluctance to make amends with Arthur. The child was an innocent victim. He had no choice but to care for her.

Last week, his greatest concern had been which mistress to choose. Now he was faced with caring for his brother's child, dealing with his mother, *and* avoiding the sensations that Miss Leybourne stirred every time she was near, at all costs. Could this Yuletide get any worse?

A high-pitched yip echoed from down the hall, answering his unspoken question.

"Your Grace, I have a letter for you from Miss Clara's mother." Mrs. Holloway reached into the pocket of her skirt and pulled out a worn envelope.

Greystone took the letter. As he began to read it, guilt coursed through his veins as his chest tightened.

Your Grace,

It is with great reluctance I prepare to leave this world and my most precious daughter. I trust you to do what's right by my sweet Clara. Against my wishes, your brother wanted you to bring her up in the event something happened to me. It was his dying wish, and one that I will honor.

I am sorry to have caused you such pain all those years ago. It will give you great satisfaction to know that ever since Arthur died, I too have suffered. He was the love of my life. Clara is so like him and has been my greatest joy. Please put aside your hatred for me.

Your humble sister-in-law,

Olive Winslow

Greystone crumpled the letter and shoved it into his pocket. Too many recessed emotions were bubbling to the surface, all vying for his attention. He would have none of it.

He swallowed the hard lump in his throat. This was family business and nothing more. "Thank you for escorting Miss Winslow. You will be compensated for your loyalty, Mrs. Holloway."

The older woman nodded uncertainly. She looked as if she wanted to say something, probably wanted to scold him, but instead chose to hold her tongue. *Wise woman.*

He'd made a mess of this evening. After arranging accommodation and early morning travel for Mrs. Holloway, he decided he needed to apologize to Patience—no, he mustn't think of her in such a familiar way—Miss Leybourne—for his behavior earlier. Despite his own trepidations, he should not have yelled at her, and he definitely should not have almost kissed her. Her honest assessment of him, although unsolicited, had given him pause. Something had changed; he no longer—or at least, not quite as much—suspected her of having ulterior motives, but he was treading on thin ice, nonetheless.

Let's get this over with. He wasn't any good at apologies and did not fancy having to make this one.

Although the festivities were still in full swing when he entered the ballroom, Miss Leybourne was nowhere to be found. He didn't know if he was relieved or annoyed that his apology would have to wait till later.

Keeping to the rear of the ballroom, he watched his mother, ensconced with his newly acquired niece and the little girl's dog, eating treats. They were giggling while the dog sat, his tail frantically wagging, mesmerized by the cake in Clara's hand. Mother pulled something out of a napkin and held it out to the little animal, who devoured it within moments.

What happened next really puzzled Greystone.

Clara threw her arms around his mother and kissed her cheek. How could that be? They'd only just met and yet somehow this little girl, and her dog, had wiggled their way into Mother's heart.

An odd sensation tingled in his own. He did not like what this scene was doing to his insides. He needed to escape…quickly.

Turning on his heel, he began the long descent along dark corridors to an even darker room which would drown out the bitter memories.

He'd reached the corridor that led to the family wing when the soft flicker of candlelight caught his attention. Who would be in the library at this hour?

His body instantly heated as he peered inside. Of course, it had to be Miss Leybourne, looking far too enticing standing on her tiptoes, reaching up for a book, exposing the gentle turn of her ankle. Her blue silk dress clung to her luscious curves. He flexed his fingers, desperate to relieve the desire to touch.

Should he leave?

No. He wanted to apologize for his earlier behavior. And besides, his desire to stay had nothing to do with the fact that Miss Leybourne's boldness both enticed and infuriated him. And it certainly had nothing to do with all the wants and cravings she stirred within him.

Not wanting to startle her, he gently cleared his throat.

She peered over her shoulder. "Oh, it's you," she said as she turned around. "You need not worry that I will steal anything, Your Grace. The hour is still rather early and I'm not in the mood for merriment. I was only searching for something to read." Her snide tone was a reminder of his earlier behavior.

"It had not crossed my mind." That was actually the truth. He'd been thinking of far more inappropriate things.

She turned around, both hands on her hips, and confronted him. "Oh, I stand corrected." She laid the sarcasm on thick. "Then I must be trying to find a book on how to land myself a duke."

Her wit was as sharp as her tongue. "I did not come here to argue."

"Then why did you come in here, *Your Grace*?"

"Why are you using such a tone?" No one had ever spoken to him thusly. He was the seventh Duke of Greystone. He deserved…no, he demanded respect, and time and time again, she had spoken her mind with no thought for consequence.

"Since your arrival, you have made your distain for me quite clear, *Your Grace*."

For reasons he couldn't explain, the formal use of his title was driving him mad. "Why must you continue to call me *Your Grace* in such a way?"

"It is your title. Do you not demand respect and proper use of it?" How did she understand him so well, when he was not even currently sure of himself? He gave her a stern look, which she challenged. "What *should* I call you then?" She held her ground, a quality he greatly admired.

He didn't know how to answer that. No one, except his mother, dared to call him anything less than Greystone. And yet, whenever he was near Miss Leybourne, he yearned to hear a sweeter endearment from her beautiful full lips.

Attempting to shake those thoughts from his mind, he cleared his throat and focused on propriety. "Your Grace is sufficient."

He turned to walk away when he heard Patience whisper under her breath, "Exactly as I thought." Although her words were soft, mockery screamed through the room.

He whipped around and stormed to where she was standing. "What's that supposed to mean?" he growled out with more anger than he'd intended. Much to her credit, she did not flinch, quite the contrary in fact.

Raising her perfect chin, she held his gaze. "That you are arrogant, and your title means *everything* to you, *Your Grace*."

Why was she goading him?

"You know nothing of what anything means to me."

"I know you think less of those beneath you—" She continued to rattle off what was wrong with him—most of which was true. But all he could think about was kissing that delectable mouth, and having Miss Leybourne *beneath* him, whispering his name in pleasure.

Damn, he had to get out of here.

Without thought of manners, he turned to leave, but only managed to take two steps when Miss Leybourne interrupted his flight once again.

"I am not finished speaking to you." His heart jolted at her words.

But he had very much finished talking to her. Two strides and he had her pressed against the bookshelf, his mouth quieting all talking. It was his body's turn to talk. To show her what he wanted.

The moment their mouths met, something exploded inside him. Patience's sharp intake of breath and exploratory hands told him that she felt the same.

Kissing her was dangerous. Kissing led to intimacy. Intimacy led to deeper feelings, which led to love. Her fiery temper had ignited every damn urge he'd buried over the past six years. He had never been so enamored by a woman before, not even…

His hand roamed over the gentle curve of her shoulder, traveling across her chest. A rapid heartbeat pounded against his hand. He dipped lower, his large palm cupping the swell of one ample bosom.

What was standing in his way, stopping him from taking her right now?

Before his mind could answer that question, she broke the kiss, and slapped him hard. A sharp sting ricocheted across his face.

That was definitely a hindrance.

Her eyes were wide with shock and desire. Her chest heaved with each word she spoke. "I told you before, you will not treat me as one of your…your mistresses." Her words said one thing, but the look in her eyes told an entirely different story.

"I have no intention making you my mistress. I thought…" How was he to express himself when he really had no idea what was going on?

"I will not allow you to reduce me to the level of whore."

"Patience, please…" She turned a violent stare on him before storming from the room. Perhaps it was for the best.

CHAPTER 6

Patience ran away as fast as she could. Her face—and other parts—still burned from where his hand had touched her. And then he'd kissed her. He'd kissed her, and she'd slapped him. She flexed her stinging hand which still ached.

A torrent of confusing emotions raged through her body.

She had enjoyed the kiss, had dreamed of him kissing her like that for the past couple of months. That wasn't the problem. His Grace had not only disappeared at Lady Trumble's ball, he hadn't sought her out after that. And then upon his arrival at Castle Greystone, he had not shown any interest in her, had been quite rude actually. And now, for no apparent reason—except that he probably always got his way—he'd kissed her. Well, she'd have none of that. She was all too familiar with the ways of rakes to succumb to his seduction. She had more pressing matters on her mind than *His Grace*.

She came face to face with an elegant white painted door inlayed in gold. *Please be better*. She offered a silent prayer.

She knocked softly before entering her aunt's chamber with caution. Images of her mother lying perfectly still, waiting for death, threatened to swallow her whole. Her chest constricted. *Be strong*.

She swallowed the hard lump in her throat and sniffled back tears, strolling into her aunt's chamber with feigned nonchalance. "Are you feeling any better this evening?" Aunt Agnes had missed Christmas dinner last night, and the festivities of Boxing Day.

"As a matter of fact, I am." Aunt Agnes *did* sound better.

The breath Patience hadn't realized she'd been holding eased out, taking with it some of the tension she had been experiencing since her aunt had been taken ill. All of a sudden, things did indeed seem brighter.

"Were you worried, dearie?"

She would have had a hard time lying to her aunt, so she settled on a half-truth. "A little." It was quite a bit more than a little, especially after everything that had happened to her mother.

"Well, Dr. Mosby said I should be good as right within a week."

"A week?" Patience tried to hide her horror that it would take that long for her aunt's recovery. She swallowed hard again, a nuisance habit that was getting worse. "That's excellent news."

"Tell me what you've been doing to occupy your time?"

She chattered on about handing out gifts, the arrival of the Duke—and subsequent removal of all the decorations, Clara's unexpected existence—which came as a complete surprise to Aunt Agnes—the weather, and anything else she could think of…everything but that kiss.

Oh, heaven help her. Just the thought of his lips on hers made her warm all over. And the way his hand cupped… Heat rose in her cheeks as her body tingled with remembrance.

"Are you ill?" Aunt Agnes questioned, interrupting her inappropriate thoughts.

"No, I…I suppose I'm just tired."

"Well, have a good rest and you can tell me more about what you've been up to tomorrow. Good night, dearie."

She brushed a kiss to the older woman's forehead. "Good night, Aunt Agnes."

WITH CLARICE PREOCCUPIED by the arrival of her granddaughter, and Aunt Agnes—although doing better—still too weak to venture from her room quite yet, Patience had decided to hide in her own room all day with her favorite book, a far better companion than His Grace. But as dinner neared, she knew the time had come to face him.

She plopped down on the ornate vanity chair and stared at her reflection in the mirror. How was she to face *him* after that kiss? She tucked a loose strand of hair behind her ear and sighed. She wished her sister were here. Parnell was calm and practical, with sage advice. Parnell would never yell at a duke, or scold him, or even slap him. Patience had really made a mess of things.

She was at a loss but could not dilly-dally any longer. She wanted to look in on her aunt before dinner.

A few minutes later, she sucked in her breath, stamping down the turmoil that was surely showing on her face and entered her aunt's suite.

"You look much better this evening."

"Thank you, dearie, I feel better." The crisp pink hue to her aunt's cheek signaled that her illness was coming to a close. In a short time, they would be able to depart Castle

Greystone and Patience could concentrate on forgetting His Grace and the unwanted feelings he stirred.

"Perhaps tomorrow you will be able to venture from your room."

"I do hope so. Being ill is rather tiresome and there are only so many needlepoints a person can complete without succumbing to boredom. And besides, I don't want to miss the Twelfth Night fête Clarice is hosting." Aunt Agnes tsked several times with disappointment. "It is a shame the house won't be decorated for that."

It most definitely is. The wheels began to turn in Patience's head before being interrupted by her aunt's rambling commentary.

"Clarice informed me that Lord Kinsley and Lady Elliot will be in attendance this evening. I'm sure you will enjoy Lord Kinsley's company, he's quite an agreeable gentleman. However, I feel the need to warn you about Lady Elliot. She can be quite the gossip. At least her daughter won't be accompanying them. Although she lives nearby, I believe she is still in mourning."

"You have nothing to fret about. I'm sure Lady Elliot will behave herself in His Grace's presence." He was a force to be reckoned with, that much she would admit. She'd learned that first hand and did not envy the person who received his full wrath. If Lady Elliot was as Aunt Agnes said, Patience would not be His Grace's focal point for contentiousness. Perhaps the evening wouldn't be so terrible after all.

She bid her aunt good night and casually strolled toward the parlor, in no rush to begin the evening's social requirements. She assumed everyone would have begun to gather in the parlor, but then firm whispers reached her ears as she passed a doorway. She was going to walk by quickly when she heard His Grace scolding his mother.

"Why did you invite them?" That seemed to be his standard question. Clearly the Duke disliked socializing with people.

"Since Lord Elliot's passing several years ago, she often dines here. If you frequented—"

"And her daughter?" Greystone interrupted. "Who else have you invited?"

"Lord Kinsley."

"Mother," he whispered under his breath.

"He's your friend, and besides, you've not exactly been cordial to Miss Leybourne. Kinsley will be much better company for her."

Patience heard a loud huff from the Duke. "I've been pleasant enough."

It was Patience's turn to let out a slight huff, *pleasant enough, indeed.*

She had heard enough. She retreated down the hall in the opposite direction. She would find another way to the parlor.

After taking a wrong turn and getting lost in the numerous connecting corridors, she finally found the correct room. A handful of guests had already gathered and, after formal introductions, dinner was called. Patience was more than pleased to be paired with Lord Kinsley. He was charming, handsome, and an excellent conversationalist, but as dinner progressed, her joy diminished.

Mrs. Mullens, who had recently come out of mourning, was making quite a spectacle of herself, peppering Greystone with questions about his various titles, followed by the sprawl of his numerous estates, and finally ending with whether he would like a large brood of children. Patience would not be surprised if the widow proposed to Greystone before the end of the evening.

Greystone's harsh narrow glare silenced any further

inquiries from Mrs. Mullens, who sat quite silently now—at least for the moment.

Unfortunately, Lady Elliot decided silence was not becoming, and turned to Patience, "I understand that your *younger* sister recently married?"

"Yes," Patience replied, then turned her attention to the venison. She would not give Lady Elliot the satisfaction of providing any more information than that which was politely required.

But even her curt reply would not deter the other woman's gossiping. "A duke, I believe, and quite the scandalous engagement," Lady Elliot stated with a sly smile, as if implying Parnell's virtue had had to be salvaged. She tapped her plump cheek with a chubby finger. "What *is* his name?"

"The Duke of Bedford." Patience was trying her best not to lose her temper and cause a scene.

And then His Grace inquired with an astonishment Patience found almost laughable. *Almost.* "Your sister married Bedford?"

"Yes."

"Your sister married the Duke of Bedford?" His Grace questioned again.

Good grief!

"Yes. My sister, nee Miss Parnell Leybourne, married His Grace, the Duke of Bedford, earlier this month, and they are currently on their wedding tour."

Greystone continued to shake his head. Patience thought she would scream if he asked her again whom her sister had married.

He looked as if he was going to speak again, when Lady Elliot looked her way and maliciously inquired, "And are you in the market for a duke as well, Miss Leybourne?"

Patience had had enough of this game. "I am not interested in marrying a duke. Any duke."

Several gasps echoed around the room, before Mrs. Mullens chimed in, "How could you not want to marry a duke?"

"I am not interested in a title. I am not interested in wealth. I do not care if my perspective husband is a duke or a farmer."

"*A farmer*?" Lady Elliot snickered. "You can't possibly be serious, Miss Leybourne."

Deep green eyes clouded in mystery—and perhaps even a little guilt—settled on her. What could she have said that would earn such a look from Greystone?

"I'm quite serious. What matters most to me is love."

"That is most honorable, my dear."

Clarice's words were interrupted by His Grace cold-hearted reflection. "Love is a fleeting affection that can turn sour in the blink of an eye."

~

AFTER A MISERABLE EVENING in the company of two of the most obnoxious women Patience had ever met, she managed to slip away when the men adjourned for brandy. She'd thought a good night's sleep would set her to rights, but her imagination tormented her with images of Her Grace standing in a stark white, empty room, surrounded by shredded decorations, crying. By morning, she was in a foul mood.

She'd had enough of *His Grace's* antics. The Dowager Duchess of Greystone had wanted the house to be festive for Christmastide and that's exactly what she intended to do. She did not care if *His Grace* tore down and discarded the decorations each night. She would simply redecorate the next morning, and every morning, until it was time to depart Castle Greystone. She would not let *His Grace* get the better of her. No, she would not. Not here in the country, not in the city. She would not, could not. Patience would have the last word.

With her mind made up and courage in place, Patience went in search of Clarice to ask permission to redecorate. She had just rounded the corner when the sound of a little child crying echoed from down the hall.

She slowed her pace and listened for which direction the sound was coming from. Soft sniffles drifted out from the open parlor door. She edged inside the dark cold room. She could hear Clara sniffing but could not see where the child was hiding. She went to the window and pulled the drapes back. Warm sunlight brushed against her cheek.

"Oh!" A small whisper escaped from behind a rose-colored settee.

Patience walked over to where the little girl was curled up behind the sofa. Max's tail went wild when he saw her. She knelt down to pet the dog as she asked Clara, "Are you alright?"

Two sniffles and a long sigh later, the little girl nodded and then shook her head.

"Perhaps I can help," Patience offered with a smile she hoped would ease the child's fear.

Clara nodded her head as she wiped away the tears.

"Would you care to sit on the sofa? Or perhaps in the chair by the window? The view is quite lovely." At the second suggestion, Clara nodded enthusiastically.

She stood and grasped Patience's hand. With Max following close behind, they went over to a pair of beautiful floral chintz chairs that overlooked a breathtaking view of the countryside.

Patience took a seat and then waited for the little girl to

take the other. Clara stood perfectly still and stared at her. Patience was not sure what to do or say. Max had no qualms about finding the perfect spot in a strip of sunlight that filtered in on the elegant carpet.

The silence drew on until Clara asked in a shy voice, "May I sit with you?"

Patience was taken aback by the request. She had only just met this little girl, and His Grace would find it entirely improper. *His Grace*. She was tired of thinking of *him* and of all the mixed emotions he constantly stirred.

Improper or not, she intended to comfort the child. "Yes."

Clara hopped up onto her lap and settled her head against Patience's chest. The scent of sweet peas drifted into her senses. "Mama would always let me sit on her lap, 'specially when I was sad."

Patience's heart lurched with an overwhelming pain that she hadn't felt since the day her mother died. Hot tears pooled in the corner of her eyes. She swallowed the hard, painful lump in her throat and tried to focus on Clara. "And what has you so upset?"

"I'm scared." The little girl's own tears streamed down her cheek as she took in huge gulps of air that wracked her entire petite body.

Another sharp pang ricocheted in her heart. "Why?"

"I'm all alone." She nestled further into Patience's embrace. "My mama and papa are gone."

Patience knew all too well the pain of losing a parent, and the desperation of not knowing whether you were alone, if you would survive, and if the pain would ease with time.

"You're not alone," she tried to reassure Clara. "You have a grandmother and an uncle." Patience was not going to add that His Grace was not a very caring person. She stroked

Clara's soft dark curls and kissed the top of her head. "My parents are gone too."

"Did you cry a lot?" Oh, dear, the little girl's words were going to be her undoing.

"Yes, and sometimes…I still cry." The confession rushed from her mouth. She blinked away the tears that threatened anew. She'd never admitted that to anyone else, not even her sister. But somehow it was important for her to share her feelings with this small angel.

Clara lifted her head and stared at Patience, her green eyes wide with shock. "You do?"

Patience nodded her head as she bit the soft flesh of her inner cheek, praying to keep the tears at bay.

Clara rested her head once again on Patience's chest. The pleasant scent of a freshly bloomed sweet peas tickled her senses again. "Are you my friend?"

"Always," Patience replied as she rested her cheek against the little girl's soft curls. "Always."

GREYSTONE HAD HEARD CRYING and assumed it was Clara. How would he ever deal with a wailing child? What would he say to her? He wasn't any good at expressing his own feelings so how was he supposed to deal with those of others, let alone a child's?

He sucked in a deep breath and prepared to enter the parlor when he heard Patience's calming voice. *"My parents are gone, too."*

He stood outside the parlor listening to Patience ease his little niece's pain.

"Did you cry a lot?" The little girl's sweet question touched him in a way he had not thought possible. Pain and something else struck his pounding heart.

"Yes, and sometimes...I still cry." But whereas Clara's question had warmed his heart, Patience's response nearly broke it.

When he was young, he'd always imagined he would marry and have a family of his own. It had been one of his greatest desires until he was deceived by Olive. His dreams had been shattered and every desire to marry had died the day he'd seen his brother swiving her like a common tavern whore. Worse had been what she said. "I only pursued you because my father wanted me to be a Duchess." She had been prepared to marry him and take his own brother as a lover, but even worse than her betrayal was his brother's. Arthur had stood by her side, choosing Olive over his family.

And here he was, watching his brother's daughter and the woman who seemed resistant to him, sharing an intimate moment.

A torrent of emotions crashed through him. His heart pounded against his chest, threatening to burst through. He needed to escape, to think, to figure out this surge of want and need and...hope.

CHAPTER 7

Patience's eyes burned, and her body ached from lack of sleep. She did not think the morning would ever come after spending an anxious night with the covers pulled over her head. A gale had rattled the windows and rumbled through her room. She detested the howling wind; it always reminded her of the night her mother had died.

Rubbing her sore neck, she walked to the window. The landscape was saturated, the trees weighed down from the torrential rain, some branches fallen, but the sky…the sky revealed patches of brilliant blue. She inhaled deeply, her lungs filling with hope. Puffy pink clouds sat on the horizon, the sun edging its way up behind them.

By the time she had completed her morning toilette and ventured outside, more dark clouds had encroached, resting on the horizon and threatening to chase away the joy of a pleasant winter's day. She realized she might have an hour in the glorious sunlight before she would have to retreat inside. Best to make the most of it.

The mild air left by the storm was a soothing balm,

chasing away the ill-effects of the night. She traversed across the footbridge that led to a Grecian temple, enjoying the splendor of nature.

Soon, her thoughts strayed to her mother's last Christmas, before the illness, before tragedy had struck her family. Patrick had helped Father bring in the Yule log while Parnell played the pianoforte. Patience had sat within the folds of her mother's warm embrace on the sofa. It had been the single most wonderful moment of her life. They were all together and happy. Then her mother had become sick and their lives had been turned upside down.

Seeing her mother lying still, all the color and life drained from her face, had devastated Patience, who had been barely fourteen. But that had been only the beginning. It was the first time she had ever seen her father in his cups. He had been barely able to hold his head up, so consumed was he with grief.

A pang struck her heart with such force that she gripped the fabric at her chest, hoping, praying, her heart would settle. Uncontrollable tears rushed down her face.

"Are you ill, Miss Leybourne?"

"Ah!" Patience let out a little scream as she faced His Grace. She didn't think it possible but the pounding in her heart had grown. She swallowed hard, attempting to regain her breath. "Yes...no. Please go away." She turned, not wanting him to see how upset she'd become.

He stepped closer.

"Please," she began on a choked whisper, "just let me alone." She wiped the tears away, but the sting was still there.

A warm hand cupped her shoulders, and that was her undoing. A torrent of emotions and tears consumed her. She did not know how it happened, but she found herself nestled into Greystone's warmth, crying into his chest. His large hand caressed her back. She was certain he offered some soothing endearments, but they were lost in the sea of her grief.

After countless minutes, he lifted her chin and looked into her eyes. There was something different about him. Not on the outside, but within. There was a gentleness in his gaze that she did not expect to find. There were so many secrets hidden within those depths, but at present, she saw only caring and compassion.

"Let me take away the pain."

The Duke began to lower his head. Should she push him away? No, definitely not. She leaned in, desperate to feel more, to experience more.

His warm breath stroked her cool cheek. His lips were so close, yet still too far away. The anticipation was killing her, but before she could protest at the distance, he brushed a soft kiss across her lips before pulling back and staring into her eyes. He seemed just as confused as she.

Within seconds, the confusion was gone and replaced with searing desire as he bent his head and took her lips in another kiss. He pulled her closer, deepening the kiss. Velvet tongues danced, enticed. It was the most glorious feeling in the world.

The dampness of the day disappeared with the fire of their kiss.

Greystone was not cold and hard, or made of stone. He was warm and muscular, very much a man. His hand traveled down the length of her back, settling on the curve of her hip. She leaned in, desperate to close the distance, desperate to feel more. Passion and desire raced through her veins. She'd never experienced anything quite like this before. No wonder ladies swooned over rakes.

All too soon, he slowed the kiss. His hand cupped her cheek as he studied her. Silence lingered between them as their bodies fought for control. Part of her was afraid of the words that would come out of her mouth if she were able to speak: *Kiss me again.*

He pulled her shawl about her shoulders and then offered his arm. "We should be returning before my mother sends the hounds after me. She believes that I might flee at any moment."

"Will you?"

He looked down into her eyes, heat and desire shining bright. "I think I might have found a reason to stay."

ONCE THEY'D RETURNED to the house, duty called Greystone away. Patience didn't know what to make of everything. When they were alone he was passionate and caring, but the moment anyone was around, he became distant, and not just with her.

Tonight's meal was the first since Greystone had arrived that Aunt Agnes was well enough to attend. Even Clara was allowed to stay up late and join the family for the intimate dinner. Thankfully, no other guests had been invited. What with her aunt's continuous—and extremely lively—flow of questions about everything she'd missed since taking ill, Clara feeding Max under the table, and Greystone staring at Patience from across the table under Clarice's questioning gaze, Patience was on edge. She'd still had not had a moment alone with Greystone to discuss that kiss.

By the time dinner had ended and they'd retired to the parlor, Patience's insides were beyond knotted. She needed answers. A man did not kiss like that and not mean it, or perhaps she was reading too much into it, just like she had at the ball. Her heart sank. She was slowly losing her heart to Greystone. Her spirits plummeted even further with the realization that he would never feel the same, probably never allow himself to feel anything more than attraction, and she would not settle for anything less than love.

Clara's voice broke through her musings. "What do you think, Miss Patty?" Clara had decided that 'Miss Leybourne' was too formal and instead informed Patience that she looked like a Miss Patty.

"It is a lovely sketch. What kind of bird is it?"

Without even pausing, the little girl responded, "It is an eagle that will carry me up to the sky." She picked up her pencil and added a cloud.

"That's far away from the ground. What's up in the sky?" Patience adored Clara's imagination and all the things the child said.

"Mama said Papa went up into the sky, past all the clouds to heaven, and I want to visit him. Do you think Mama went to heaven, too?"

A faint snort crept from across the room. Patience looked up and saw Greystone standing in the open door.

She ignored the mocking sound and instead reassured Clara. "I'm sure she is with your papa and both are watching over you."

Clara smiled brightly as she jumped to her feet, startling Max, and gave Patience a hug. "I'm going to draw you a picture, Miss Patty."

"I can't wait to see what you create." Patience kissed Clara's cheek before the child gave Max a big hug then plopped back down on the floor and set to work on a new drawing.

"I'll be back shortly to see your progress."

Patience ignored Clarice's inquiring gaze and approached Greystone. Narrowing her eyes with displeasure, she nodded her head toward the hall, hoping he would take the hint to follow, but didn't say a word. Patience could not trust herself not to unleash her full wrath.

They had not even taken two steps into the hall when Greystone growled out, "What's this all about?"

"Not here," she whispered. Grabbing his hand, she pulled him down the dark hall. Whispering over her shoulder, she said, "I don't want her to hear us."

When she believed they had traveled far enough from earshot, she turned to face Greystone. Barely able to keep the anger from her voice, she began to scold him. "Regardless of your feelings you cannot shatter that little girl's memories."

"You know nothing of my feelings."

"It's clear that you cannot let whatever happened in the past remain in the past. You appear cold and insensitive at times."

"Really, after the kiss…" He looked around before he lowered his voice. "After the kiss we shared?"

"This isn't about that kiss. And besides, I know how you feel about love. You stated your position quite clearly." He opened his mouth to speak, but she held up her hand to keep him from speaking. "This is about Clara and all that she's suffered. She lost both parents and now finds herself in your care."

"WHY ARE you so protective of Clara?" The words shot from his mouth without thought.

Patience seemed taken aback by the question. Truth be told, he was too.

Her blue eyes were full of sadness, warmth, and compassion. "I know what it's like to have lost both parents. The pain never leaves." She inhaled a shaky breath. "And the gossip only makes it worse."

"I…I'm sorry." Greystone didn't know what to say, and worse, his half-arsed apology sounded weak, even to his own ears.

"It's not your fault." Patience worried her bottom lip. In that moment, he wanted to take away all her pain and heartache.

"Patience," he breathed out, hoping she wouldn't pull away from him.

"Your Grace," she murmured.

In a moment of pure insanity, he offered what he had *never* offered to anyone before. "Theodore."

She seemed hesitant at first, and when her lips parted, it felt like an eternity before she said what he longed to hear. "Theodore." His name came out on a breathy whisper.

There was no more time for words. Greystone lowered his lips to hers and brushed soft kisses along them, savoring the sweet taste of her lips. The kiss was slow, thoughtful, and surprisingly gentle, considering how desperate he was to have more. He wanted to savor the moment, never wanting it to end.

Sounds of laughter and Max barking drifted from down the hall, interrupting their interlude.

Patience pulled back out of his embrace and looked into his eyes. "Promise me that whatever may come, you will be kind and loving to Clara." Her request had a morbid undertone that darkened his joy. What could she mean? "Promise me, Theodore." Her intense stare went straight to his heart. He would have promised her the moon in that moment.

"I promise."

"Oh, there you two are." His mother's timing was impeccable. "Patience, your aunt was wondering if you would play the pianoforte before the evening comes to an end?"

"Yes, of course." Patience stepped away from him, leaving him cold and wanting.

Mother raised a quizzical brow, but thankfully kept her thoughts to herself. He was at a crossroad and he didn't know what to do.

"I believe I will retire now."

~

A COUPLE OF HOURS LATER, his mind was still at odds with what had occurred with Patience. She had stood up to him on Clara's behalf and then asked him to be kind and loving to his niece. The wall surrounding his heart was slowly crumbling and a surge of emotions was muddling his thoughts.

He pulled the stopper off the decanter and poured a healthy serving of brandy. He stared at what had become his usual form of escape over the past six years. He didn't like what he'd become.

"Damn," he swore as he tossed the glass and its contents into the dying embers. Flames rose high in the massive fireplace. He would not succumb to this poison any longer.

He flung open the door of his suite and headed toward his study. He would begin to set things to right tonight. He had assumed everyone would have retired by this hour, but as he neared the music room, a soft hum reached his ears. Halting just outside the door, he peered inside and spied Patience draping a garland of ivy and ribbon across the mantle.

"What are you doing?" Although his tone held none of the anger it had before, when Patience turned around, he could see she was ready to argue. Her next words confirmed it.

"I know you don't approve, but for Clara's—and your

mother's—sake, please let me decorate just this room. They deserve a happy festive season."

He ran a frustrated hand through his hair. "I…" He inhaled deeply, not knowing what to say. The emotions he'd been avoiding for the past six years rushed through his body, practically paralyzing him with fear and an all-consuming need that he'd been suppressing.

Patience came over to him. "I don't know all of what you suffered in the past, but can't you put that behind you and look to the future?"

The need she constantly stirred was going to be his downfall.

"I…don't know if I'm capable." The words tore from his mouth on a ragged breath.

She placed a gentle hand on his arm, leaned in, and brushed a kiss on his cheek. "You're standing under the mistletoe," she whispered.

Something snapped in his mind. The room began to spin, and he jerked away from her.

Mistletoe.

He looked up and saw, hanging in the doorway, a spray of the plant with large white berries. Images of his brother and Olive rushed to the forefront of his mind. Without thought, he reached up and tore the sprig down and tossed it to the floor.

"What are you doing?" Shock laced every syllable as the words echoed off the walls, but he could hardly discern Patience's words as the anger built inside him to epic proportions.

"I do not want my house decorated." He glared down at her. "Not now, not ever! You are not to disobey my orders."

"Do you not care for those around you?" Despite his efforts to try and move around her, she continued to plead her case. "What of your mother and Clara? They will be so disappointed."

"The world is full of disappointments. Better for Clara to learn and accept that now than to have her heart ripped from her chest by…" His words trailed off, halted by the intense beating of his heart.

"Are we speaking of Clara or you?" Crossing her arms, Patience continued to hold her ground. "You are so consumed with your own *disappointments,* as you put it, that you cannot see that there is a little girl who needs you, needs your love."

The words that he'd been trying to convince himself of for the last several years spewed from his mouth. "*Love*, hah! It is a stupid sentiment that—"

"Thank you for explaining your position." Patience looked at him in horror, as if he were an uncaring monster, but her voice was calm. "I believe I shall take my leave now."

"Patience, wait—" he called as she began to retreat down the hall.

"No. I have finished waiting. I have been waiting for years to find love, passion, and happiness." She let out a cynical laugh. "I never want to be so coldhearted. I believe your heart to be two sizes too small, *Your Grace*." She turned partway before halting and speaking over her shoulder. "I suppose I should thank you. You've opened my eyes to the world." And with that, she walked away along the dark hall, leaving a hole in his heart.

CHAPTER 8

Patience was past the point of being upset. She was livid. Every time she thought Greystone and she were growing closer, he did something to push her away. She could see the struggle in his eyes. Why wouldn't he just talk to her? Tell her what had happened to cause such angst. She paced the length of the room contemplating her next move. She felt as if she were playing a game of chess. There was only one problem; she didn't know how to play chess, and she suspected that she was losing miserably. Perhaps it was best if she left Castle Greystone. She inhaled deeply, contemplating that decision.

Knock, knock.

She swirled around. Who could it be at this hour? Another very soft knock sounded.

She opened the door, half expecting to see her aunt. "Clara? What's the matter?"

The little girl clutched her blanket as she edged into the room, followed by Max. "May I sleep in your bed, Miss Patty?"

Patience bent down and picked up the little girl, the fresh

scent of sweet peas encircling her once more. For the rest of her life this scent would always remind her of Clara. Her heart ached with the thought of never seeing the child again.

Clara rested her head against her shoulder. "I love you."

Oh, my. She swallowed the despair in her throat as she clutched the girl. "I love you, too."

No sooner had she set Clara down on the bed then Max jumped up and claimed his spot at its foot. Within minutes Clara had nestled into her and fallen asleep. She spent the next few hours wondering what she was going to do.

~

Greystone trudged into the breakfast room still reflecting on the mess of things he'd made last night, and all because he could not come to terms with the past and the woman who'd run off with his brother and broken his heart. Some wounds ran too deep to be healed.

"Theodore, have you seen Clara this morning?"

"No, the child is probably still abed."

"She's not in her room, and neither is Max." His mother took a slice of cake before taking her seat at the breakfast table. "Perhaps she's with Patience. She hasn't been down this morning either."

"I'm not Miss Leybourne's keeper," he snapped out.

His mother gave him a dubious look. "I didn't say you were." She added milk to her tea and began to stir, the spoon never touching the sides of the cup. "I was only inquiring. She has not been to visit her aunt today."

"Perhaps she was in need of some quiet time." Much like he was at the moment.

"You do not need to be curt with me." She placed the spoon down on the saucer to her cup none too softly. "I am still your mother and expect respect." Avoiding eye contact, she pushed away from the table abandoning her tea, clearly angry with her son.

"Where are you going?"

"Nowhere that concerns you." She tossed the words about, but still did not glance his way. He didn't want to leave things as they were. He knew Mother would fester with feelings of hurtfulness and anger all day and then break down in tears. He did not want to be the one responsible for that…again.

He stood and within two strides was at her side. "Mother, I'm sorry. I have much on my mind and—"

"I have my own duties to see to." She began to move past him. He suspected there was more to this conversation and he meant to get to the bottom of it.

"Such as?"

"*Such as* discovering where Clara and Patience have disappeared to."

Why did their conversation always seem to return to Miss Leybourne? Wasn't it bad enough that she had invaded his home and his thoughts, challenged every word, and made him want to believe in hope?

He looked down at his mother, about to say as much, when he noticed the genuine concern on her face. "Why are you so bothered about her?"

Mother huffed out an indelicate *humph*. "It is not like her to miss a visit to her aunt in the morning."

"Perhaps she went for a walk with Clara."

"Don't be ridiculous. Have you not noticed it has been raining for the past hour?"

He was about to offer another explanation when Boris entered the room. "Pardon me, Your Grace. I have been informed by Miss Leybourne's maid that Miss

Winslow and Max are still abed in Miss Leybourne's room."

Greystone turned to his mother. "You see, the mystery of Clara's whereabouts is solved. She is with Miss Leybourne."

The butler cleared his voice. "Actually, Miss Leybourne has not been seen for a couple of hours. Her maid said she went for an early morning walk and has yet to return."

Greystone felt the life drain out of him. What if she was in danger? "Go and check on Clara, and I'll search for Patience," he barked out as he left the room. Icy cold fear shivered down his spine as he headed for the stables. He had to find her.

"Did Miss Leybourne come this way?" he called to one of the stablemen.

"I saw her walking toward the Grecian temple, but that was a couple of hours ago."

"Ready my horse."

After what felt like an hour later, he set off in the direction of the temple. What was Patience thinking, traversing the grounds on a day like this? Clearly, she was lacking common sense.

That thought did not sit well with him. She had more common sense than the average person. As of late, she was probably in possession of more of it than he was. Damn, what was he going to do with her?

He pondered this question as he rode away from the house. There was no sign of her anywhere. He called out her name several times but was only met with the pitter-patter of rain disturbing the otherwise peaceful countryside.

Nearly a half an hour later, he was about to turn back and gather reinforcements when he spotted a shape approaching in the far distance. As the rider neared, he realized there wasn't just one person on horseback, but two.

He squinted at the pair, and they slowly came into focus.

Patience and Kinsley. She was seated in front of him.

The chill in his veins melted away as his blood began to boil, and another betrayal rang in his ears. A slur of accusations rested on his tongue as the pair approached.

By the time they reached him, his hands were strangling the reins of his own mount, the whites of his knuckles straining against taut skin.

"Where have you been?" he growled out to Patience, ignoring his one-time friend.

"I…I went for a w…walk," she began to chatter between shivers, "…and I g…got lost."

"It's true—" Kinsley began before Greystone cut him off with a harsh glare. He was in no mood to listen to their lies.

Patience quickly—too quickly in his opinion—came to Kinsley's defense. "L…Lord Kinsley found me w…wandering by the stream."

"I'll take Miss Leybourne back to the castle." Without any further acknowledgement, Greystone pulled Patience off Kinsley's lap and seated her in front of him, adjusted his coat around her, and then nudged Karl away from a stunned Kinsley.

"Th…that was rude," Patience ground out with a shiver.

"We will discuss it later."

Except for the chatter of Patience's teeth, the ride passed in silence. But inside, Greystone was fuming, his temper reaching epic proportions.

No sooner had he brought Karl to a halt than Patience slid off the horse and was giving him a piece of her mind. "I cannot believe that you would treat Lord Kinsley in such a manner. He only offered his assistance, nothing more."

"Yes, I am very well aware of what kind of assistance the bastard is capable of offering." He dismounted his horse and tossed the reins to the groom. He would have preferred to have this discussion inside, behind closed doors, but Patience was of a different opinion.

She gave him a hostile stare as she spat out the words contemptuously, "What have I done to earn such distrust? I'm not Olive. I've never tried to deceive you."

"How do you know about her?" He stopped dead in his tracks.

"Lord Kinsley."

"He had no right—"

"He had every right since you won't discuss a damn thing. Since you arrived, you have done nothing but confuse me. You tore down the Christmas decorations…twice, you implied that I was duke-hunting, that I somehow tricked your mother into inviting me, and then you kissed me. What do you want from me?"

"I don't know." It was the grandest lie the century had ever heard, but he *was* not going to tell her the truth.

"I see." A strange calm entered her voice. "Thank you for sharing your mother and niece with me during Christmastide. I believe it best that I take my leave now." She began to stroll away.

"What is that supposed to mean?" he called after her.

Patience did not turn back or acknowledge him in any way but kept walking straight toward the house.

What had he done?

He wanted to run away. Run from this place. Run from the memories. It was easier to run away than to deal with it all. But before he could move two feet, one of the house servants came tearing toward him.

"Her Grace has requested your presence in her parlor."

This did not bode well for him.

He entered his mother's primrose-yellow parlor, the

bright color a direct contrast to his soul, with his tail between his legs and braced himself for the lecture of a lifetime.

"Sit."

He did as he was told, taking the seat across from her, without so much as a sigh. He was a duke, but first and foremost he was a son; her son.

"I don't understand you anymore, not since Arthur ran off." It was the first time he'd heard his mother speak his brother's name since the scandal. It sounded odd and reassuring all at once. "Every time you have happiness within your grasp, you throw it away."

He opened his mouth to argue, but knew his mother was correct. He felt guilty for what had happened to his brother, and for not making amends, for letting his temper get the better of him, and letting down both his parents.

As if reading his thoughts, his mother responded, "Arthur made his choices. He chose to deceive you. He chose to run off with that woman. It was not, and is not, your fault." They had never spoken about what happened, but somehow after all these years, his mother's words were comforting.

He took in a long breath and allowed images of himself and Arthur playing as children, creating mischief as teens, and reminisces about their talks about the future, to enter his thoughts. It was the first time in six years he'd allowed those kinds of recollections to enter his mind.

The wall around his heart began to crumble. He missed his brother.

"Did you love Olive, *really* love her?"

He searched the darkest parts of his soul. The answer had always been there, but he'd been too wounded by deception to admit the truth. The answer was clear, simple.

"No."

Mother stood and walked up to him. She grabbed his chin

with warm, delicate fingers and turned his head toward her. "Now, what happened with Patience, that *was* your fault."

"Sh…she told you?"

"No. I saw her enter the house from my window. She was crying."

The sting of her words careened through the rubble and went straight to his heart.

"I am no expert, but I know love when I see it. You love her, and she loves you. She cares about Clara. Regardless of the past, that child is your responsibility now." Her gaze was direct and unwavering. "Clara needs a mother and you need a wife."

"I made a mess of things," Greystone confessed as he ran a shaky hand through his hair. Admitting his failings was hard to swallow.

"I know, but there's still time to remedy that."

CHAPTER 9

Patience was thankful Greystone did not follow her inside. She didn't know if she would unleash more anger and fury or collapse in tears. Desperate to avoid prying eyes, she kept her head low and scurried along the long corridor to the grand staircase.

"Miss Leybourne?" Lord Kinsley's voice halted her flight. She sucked in a deep, trembling breath before raising her eyes. His kind sincere gaze met hers. "Are you alright?"

She shook her head. "I'm sorry at the way His Grace treated you."

"It's not your fault. That's what I came here to tell him."

"It doesn't matter. None of it matters. It is quite clear he cannot let go of the past. And, I'm leaving." Despite the confident tone she was trying to achieve, her heart constricted, begging her to reconsider.

Lord Kinsley quickly interjected, "No, you shouldn't leave. He hasn't been the same—"

Waving her hand, she halted his excuse. "Why do you defend him after his behavior toward you?"

"Because I know what happened, and I see the way he

looks at you. Ever since Lady Trumble's ball, he's been like a lovesick schoolboy. Just give him time."

Blinking away the tears stinging the corners of her eyes, she said, "I need to leave."

Much to his credit, Lord Kinsley did not try to sway her further. "Then allow me to offer my carriage."

"Thank you. I would like to depart as soon as possible."

~

Several hours later, Patience was ready. She could not wait to leave Castle Greystone. The last thing she wanted was to see *him* again. The memory of Greystone and those few perfect moments they'd shared together would, she hoped, fade into the recesses of her mind.

Why couldn't he understand that she did not care about titles and wealth, that she had no ulterior motives, that she just wanted him?

But that would never be enough.

She would not give into tears or hysterics.

After scribbling a quick note to her aunt, Patience gathered her small traveling valise, slipped out of the elegant aubergine suite of rooms, and began the long trudge of out the castle.

Save for the servants going about their daily routine, the house was quiet. She prayed her flight would go unnoticed. As she reached the Great Hall, she slowed her pace, practically tip-toeing, hoping to not make a sound.

High-pitched yips echoed through the hall moments before she saw Max rushing across the black and white marble floor toward her. She quickly dropped her bag, brought the dog within her embrace, and began to pet him.

"Shh, you don't want to disturb the whole house." The

moment she stood, the dog began to whine. "Oh, very well, just one last belly rub," she said as she bent down again. "I can't stroke you all afternoon. I have to go."

Max flipped around and came to a sitting position. He tilted his head and stared at her. She could only imagine what the dog was thinking. He'd forget about her once the evening meal was served and Clara handed him treats under the table.

She settled for one more pat on his head before grabbing her valise.

"Going somewhere?" The deep timbre of Greystone's voice reached all the way down to her toes.

She let out a long sigh as she slowly turned around. She didn't know what she was going to say, but whatever it was, she would say it quickly, then take her leave. But when she turned and met his deep green eyes, all words flew out of her mind.

"Before you scold, reprimand, or otherwise put me in my place," he paused as he strolled toward to her. "Allow me to apologize for all of my behavior. You were right about… everything." He closed the final distance, standing mere inches from her. "I lost sight of what was most important."

She stared at him, wordlessly, her heart pounding as hope soared through her entire body.

"You."

In one forward motion she was in his arms, his mouth caressing hers with sweet tenderness. It was divine ecstasy. All thoughts of leaving rushed from her mind, and besides, she truly did not want to leave. She suppressed her protest when his lips left hers.

"I have a surprise for you." He took her hand, tucking it within the fold of his arm and guided her toward the parlor.

She didn't know what to except, what with her mind being still clouded by his apology, followed by his kiss. But when she entered the parlor, the last thing she expected to see was the space completely decorated, transformed into the Christmas of her dreams.

Tears pooled in the corner of her eyes.

"Oh, my," she whispered, barely keeping all her emotions at bay.

"Do you like it?" There was a slight tinge of wonder in his voice.

Looking up into his hopeful gaze, she said without hesitation, "It's the most beautiful room I've ever seen."

Garlands of greenery intertwined with red and silver ribbon were draped across the mantle and wainscoting. Large shimmering bows adorned every nook, and fanciful streams of silver ribbon cascaded across and down the elegant side tables. Every corner of the room, every surface, was decorated.

But when she looked up and saw dozens of boughs of mistletoe hanging from the ceiling beams, tied by delicate silver ribbon, her tears streamed down her cheeks. Greystone's fingers tenderly wiped away the moisture, caressing her cheek, before shifting her chin to meet his gaze.

"The only future I fear is one without you." His lips brushed against hers as he spoke, sending delicious tingles all over her body. "Please do me the honor and say you'll be my Duchess."

My Duchess. It sounded so deliciously…perfect.

She threw her arms around his neck and kissed him with all the love she felt in her heart, savoring every moment. His hands trailed down her back, bringing her closer.

"Yes," she whispered against his lips. "Yes."

"May we come in now?" Clara's sweet voice yelled from beyond the entry.

Laughter rumbled in Greystone's chest. "Yes."

The little girl came rushing in, with Max right beside her, followed by Clarice and Aunt Agnes. A moment later, Lord Kinsley strolled into the festive room, and sauntered straight over to Patience.

"May I be the first to congratulate you on your engagement, Miss Leybourne," he said with a sincere smile.

Her look of astonishment must have shown on her face. Greystone explained, "Despite my earlier behavior, Kinsley took it upon himself to ensure I did not make another disastrous mistake." He leaned in, brushed a kiss against her ear, then whispered, "He informed me I was being an unmitigated ass."

Laughter streamed from her mouth as utter joy bubbled from within. This was the happiest of Christmastides.

EPILOGUE

December 24, 1820

Hazy sunlight drifted into the serene parlor creating an ethereal quality within the room. Greystone watched his beloved enjoying the splendor of a winter's day from the warm comfort of the beautiful parlor, which she'd recently had redecorated in soft green and white, with accents of red. Patience said she chose the color scheme because it reminded her of Christmastide and when they fell in love.

"And how are you today, my Duchess?" Greystone said as he strolled into the parlor.

"Absolutely perfect." Her smile brightened the room and warmed his heart.

He brushed a kiss across her lips before inquiring, "Are you certain you're up for this?"

She reached for his hand, encouraging him to sit beside her. "I've never felt better."

"Are you certain—"

"Oh my," she whispered as she sat forward slightly.

"What? What's the matter?" He started to stand. "Should I send for—"

Tugging on his hand to keep him from leaving, she reassured him, "The baby is kicking quite intensely this afternoon." She brought his palm to her stomach. A moment later, a firm nudge pressed against the spot where it rested.

His eyes widened. Awe and utter joy coursed through his veins. "That's our baby."

Since their Twelfth Night wedding nearly a year ago, he had come to terms with the past. He'd forgiven Arthur and Olive for their deceitfulness, and prayed his brother and sister-in-law were, at long last, at peace. He was embracing his future with Patience and Clara, and their growing family.

"They're here! They're here!" Clara's voice, along with Max's high-pitched yip, cheered through the house.

He helped Patience up, then pulled her into a warm embrace, showering kisses around her lips.

"What was that for?" she asked, a delicious pink blush staining her cheeks.

"For bringing the spirit of Christmas back into the house." He kissed the tip of her nose. "For not quite giving up on me, even when I was most determined to become a hermit." He brushed a kiss across her cheek. "For loving me." The kiss that followed was slow and enticing, sending a thousand tingles in every direction of his body. He had found his soul, his love.

"Ahem." He reluctantly eased back from the kiss to find his mother standing in the doorway. "Perhaps you did not hear," she started with a tease as laughter filled her voice, "but they're here."

He and Patience followed his mother to the sound of chatter and laughter emanating from the Great Hall as their guests arrived.

Patience's giddiness was contagious, her smile reaching

from ear to ear as she rushed toward her siblings. “I’m ecstatic you’re finally here.”

Greystone watched as she embraced her brother and sister, and their children. His heart lurched, but before the heartache of the past could creep its way back, Patience reached out her hand to his, bringing him within the folds of her family. And in that moment, he truly believed his heart had grown three sizes.

WHEN THE MARQUESS RETURNS EXCERPT

When the Marquess Returns

By Alanna Lucas

Chapter One

London, May 1819

The moment Maximus, his brother, and their adoptive mother entered the spacious hall of the grand theatre, curious eyes settled on them and murmurs encircled their small party.

Stares were commonplace whenever they entered a room, especially in this new environment. It had always been the case, although the novelty usually wore off within a couple of minutes. However, there was one lady in particular who kept her gaze centered on them, puzzlement streaked across her face. She tilted her brow, looking at them with uncertainty, almost as if she were trying to understand something. She didn't attempt to approach but continued to peer intently at them.

"Why is that woman staring at us?" Maximus questioned under his breath, barely able to keep the annoyance at bay.

"Perhaps she's never seen twins before," Lucius rebuffed.

Maximus and Lucius were not just twins, they were identical and—according to the local girls in the small village close to their childhood home near Plymouth—were "two of the most handsome men alive, and completely swoon-worthy". It was a moniker that Maximus did not care for, never had and probably never would. He'd rather be known for his intelligence, or skill with a horse, or knowledge of multiple languages, not for something as fleeting as appearance.

"Perhaps you remind her of someone. Just ignore," Larentia, their mother, said with nonchalance and a slight wave of her hand. "These women of the *ton* are often far too absorbed in gossip. Besides, we've only just arrived in Town. It couldn't possibly have anything to do with us."

"Miss St. Albans!" a cheerful voice crescendoed above the crowd bringing even further attention to their party. A rather plump woman dressed in deep purple scurried towards them. "You've finally returned to London."

"Lady Kenton," Larentia took the woman's hands in her own. "It has been too long, my dearest friend."

"Twenty-three years too long to be exact." The woman's warm smile settled on Maximus and his brother. "These must be your adopted sons. It is a pleasure to meet you both at long last. Larentia has written to me often of your adventures. Tell me, how did you enjoy your time on the Continent?"

Their time touring Europe felt like a lifetime ago. When their adoptive grandfather announced he wanted Maximus and Lucius to follow in his footsteps and embark on the Grand Tour, the brothers were just nineteen and—in Maximus's opinion—naïve about the world beyond

Plymouth. It had been a time of great personal growth for each of them. He'd enjoyed visiting new places, experiencing local customs, honing his drafting skills, and spending time with his brother, but he'd always longed for more. However, before he could conclude what 'more' encompassed, they'd been summoned home.

So much had happened since they'd returned two years ago.

"It was most enjoyable," Maximus answered in a tone he hoped did not invite further questions. He was not in the mood for reminiscing, for sharing those intimate details of their travels, with someone he'd just met.

His brother on the other hand…

"I particularly enjoyed the opera in Milan, *e le belle donne*," Lucius said before adding his infamously charming smile that quite frequently landed him in trouble.

"*Ricorda il nostro accordo*," Maximus warned under a hushed tone as Lady Kenton watched their exchange with interest. The brothers had already argued once today about Lucius's indiscretions since arriving in London a few days previous.

Lucius raised a brow in defiance, but kept his tone jovial. "*Lei non capisce l'italiano*."

"Oh my, and you both speak Italian?" A slight giggle escaped Lady Kenton's mouth as a deep blush stained her entire face. Turning back to Larentia, she said, "I have not a clue what they are saying, however, I do believe the mamas had best keep a close watch on their daughters with your sons in Town this season."

Larentia shot Maximus and Lucius her best "behave your-self" warning before clearing her throat. "The play is about to begin."

"Oh yes, and it should be quite a spectacular performance

this evening. Madame Hébert is performing the aria this evening." The trio followed Lady Kenton up the grand staircase toward her box, passing even more curious eyes. "We'll have plenty of time to get acquainted later."

The gentle hum of conversation and general merriment that had filled the theatre lessened—only slightly—as the production began. Even as Maximus tried to focus on the stage and ignore the chatter echoing across the vast gold and green space, his mind wandered, contemplating the disagreement he'd had with his brother earlier regarding Lucius's current paramour. The woman in question had actually snuck into their townhome and cornered Maximus, believing *he* was Lucius. Then, upon discovering they were identical twins, offered her services to both brothers. Maximus lost his temper with the woman, which angered his brother.

Why did he and his twin have to constantly be at odds? It never had been this way until their grandfather had passed away and they'd learned they would have to leave St. Albans Manor for London. Looking back, something had begun to change with Lucius that day.

Maximus adjusted himself for the umpteenth time, swiveling this way and that, trying to find a comfortable position. It wasn't that the seat was uncomfortable, or that he could even place blame on his surroundings—despite all the stares, it was that *he* was uncomfortable; uncomfortable and restless.

He stretched his legs and, in the process, made contact with his brother's chair. Two glaring blue eyes met his. "What is wrong with you?" Lucius's scold rumbled above the performance.

He shook his head, brushing off his brother's question. They'd already had one argument this evening, and he would be damned if they had another—and this one not in the privacy of their home. He couldn't do that to Larentia…again.

Damn. Why couldn't he relax?

He turned his focus to the stage, trying to enjoy… Hell, he couldn't even recall what he was supposed to be enjoying. A long sigh escaped his lips, earning a glare from all in their box. He attempted to adjust his legs again, this time kicking his brother's ankle. Lucius eyed him with annoyance, his mouth opened as if to argue, then he snapped it shut.

This was pointless.

Maximus left the box before he annoyed his brother further, and ducked into the hall, his muscles instantly relaxing. Perhaps he just wasn't used to the city. Except for those couple of years spent traveling across the Continent, he had spent little time in any city, much preferring quiet country life. A quick walk should ease whatever was plaguing him.

Strolling casually, ignoring the couple of theatregoers loitering at the far end of the hall, he began to make his way toward the grand staircase. Before he reached his destination, a muffled argument from one of the boxes halted his retreat.

No sooner had the sounds reached his ear when a woman stormed out of the box in question, colliding with him. He wrapped his arm about her waist to keep her from landing on the floor. They stood chest to chest, hearts beating rapidly.

"Oh," she gasped. "I…" Her words halted as she glanced up at him. Warm vanilla and sweet lavender encircled them.

Maximus stared into the most enticing eyes he'd ever seen—one emerald green, one deep brown. Her compelling eyes riveted him in place as his heart pounded against his chest anew.

Time halted, and energy surged between them. She stared at him with a tender longing.

Who was this woman?

Countless moments later, the lady spoke. "I apologize for ruining—"

"You didn't ruin anything," he quickly reassured her, but couldn't the find words to say more.

Her mouth curved into a beautiful smile, revealing matching dimples, which sent a whirlwind through his world. He'd always had a fondness for dimples. "I…I best be returning to my party."

"I suppose I should release you," he said with reluctance.

"Yes, I suppose," the words brushed past her pink lips with the same reluctance.

Several seconds passed before he actually did release her, his body instantly feeling the loss. Before he could ask her name, she retreated back into the box, leaving him wondering what the hell had just happened. If not for the remnants of lavender and vanilla clinging to his coat, he might have believed he dreamt the entire scene.

He paced a short length several times trying to convince himself he should *not* sneak into the box and discover her identity. *They had not been properly introduced. It would create a scene*. In the end, common sense won, and he decided it was best to rejoin his party.

Maximus took in a deep breath, the muscles tightening in chest, as he reluctantly walked back to his box.

"So nice of you to join us again." His brother's tone was laced with sarcasm as Maximus entered the loge. "I hope you've settled down."

His patience was being tested at every turn this evening. Before he could remark, Larentia stated, "Lady Kenton has offered to show us around Town later this week. Perhaps we may see the Egyptian Hall."

Maximus simply nodded as he took his seat. He had other things on his mind presently. He desperately wanted to discover more about the woman he'd encountered in the hall, and what had caused her to be so upset, and....

His heart sank. What if she was married and had quarreled with her husband? If that were the case, it was probably fortunate he hadn't barged in on her party. Before too long, he had conjured an entire scenario that had him enraged and wanting to call out the bastard who had upset her.

Damn. He needed to stay calm. He didn't even know her name. What if she wasn't married? How would he discover her identity without a proper introduction? He pondered the question for several minutes before an idea struck.

As soon as the play finished, he would rush to her box and casually bump into her again. It was a simple plan without the possibility of scandal. He would be able to talk to her again, and with any luck, acquire her name.

With his plan settled, he rather impatiently waited for the play to end. At least this time he knew what was disrupting his senses—a blonde-haired beauty, with the most intriguing eyes, four boxes away.

Loud clapping thundered through the theatre bringing him back to the present. Larentia and Lady Kenton were deep in conversation about the quality of the play and Madame Hébert's performance, while Lucius seemed distracted by something, or rather someone, near the stage.

Adrenaline rushed through his veins. There was no time to lose. He would worry about the next step once he found her again.

Emerging into the hall, excitement quickly gave way to frustration as his progress was hindered by several parties loitering in the hall engaging in lively talk about the evening's festivities, both on stage and in the audience. Maximus edged around them and waited near the box the lady had retreated to. With each passing minute, he became more anxious as more and more people filled the corridor. He watched as Larentia and Lady Kenton strolled past, and Lucius disappeared in the opposite direction. He could not be bothered with his brother's antics at the moment. Besides, he was his twin, not his keeper. He watched as the crowd dispersed and still no one emerged from box number four.

His insides turned as he struggled to formulate a new plan. Perhaps he could enter the loge, mistaking it for his own, claiming he'd forgotten…well, he didn't know what, he'd conjure some item when the time came. He maneuvered past the strolling guests, sucked in his breath, and pulled back the curtain.

Empty.

A heavy sigh escaped his lips. Where had she gone?

"Renovations on the cottage are almost complete. You'll finally be able to leave Warrington Hall."

"I enjoy spending time with Lady March," Sabina corrected her brother. Plus, she couldn't imagine being alone day after day, removed from Warrington Hall and those she held dear.

Titus ignored her comment, continuing on to extol the positives of the renovation. "I believe you will be most pleased with the small library," he said with much enthusiasm.

Since her lifelong dream to marry and have a family of her own would never be, it was nice to know that she would have a lovely cottage, far away from the gossips, to call her own. Despite her circumstances, she still fared better than most spinsters, thanks to her brother. He might be several years younger than her, but once he reached his majority, he had always ensured her future was secure.

Before she could express her appreciation for what Titus

had arranged, her sister-in-law—Eunice, interfered. "The final steps into spinsterhood," she said with a snicker. "And a fitting end for the Cursed Heiress."

"Eunice, that's enough," Titus half-scolded. Sabina could not blame her brother for not taking a firmer approach with his wife. He had to endure her—and their mother—every day he took a breath, not to mention still being in need of an heir. She truly felt for him.

"You shouldn't take that tone with your wife," their mother said as she took Eunice's hand, lovingly folding it within her own.

Eunice raised a triumphant chin before taking another jab at Sabina's expense. "I suppose living the life of a spinster in the old hunting cottage *is* better than being at Lady March's side constantly." Eunice clearly had learned the disagreeable art of insulting Sabina from her husband's mother. For two women not related, the similarities and jibes were endless.

As if enduring her sister-in-law wasn't trying enough, Mother decided it was her turn to chime in, "I still can't quite comprehend how you managed to swindle His Grace and Lady March into letting you reside with them all these years."

Mustering what little bravado she had left in her soul, Sabina retorted, "Perhaps if you had been more—"

Mother's eyes turned ice cold and filled with hatred. "What? More of a mother?" She clutched her hand to her chest, her performance rivaling those of the actors on stage. "I was grieving the loss of my husband."

"And my father." Sabina shook her head, trying to erase the memory of that horrible day and her mother's unkind words. She did not want to suffer another lecture, followed by an argument, and conclude with more insults. Instead she settled for a plea. "I rarely see you and Titus. Do you not think it possible that we could have a pleasant evening just this once, Mother?"

"I agree with Sabina." For the second time that evening, her brother came to her defense, but she was certain he would pay the price later.

"Of course, you do," cried Eunice. "You always side with your *dearest* sister. You don't care for me." Sniffling, she buried her face in her hands.

Or sooner it would seem.

"There, there, Eunice, darling." Sabina's mother, the woman who'd given birth to her, who was supposed to love her, was comforting the instigator. Mother raised her gaze to Sabina. "Look what you've done." Hatred blazed in her eyes. "What have *I* done to deserve a daughter like you? I've been cursed since the day you were born."

The words seared straight through Sabina's heart, striking at her very core. Tears burned the corners of her eyes as she fought to control her breathing. One would think she would be used to the barbs after enduring so many years of them, but they still hurt. Since her father's passing, all she had ever wanted was her mother's love.

Desperate to escape, even if only for a moment to regain her composure, Sabina swallowed the hard lump in her throat, raised her chin, pulled back the curtain, rushed from their box none-too-gracefully, and straight into a wall. Only this wall was warm and smelled like a pleasant autumn afternoon in the country.

Firm arms wrapped about her waist, keeping her from falling. She glanced up into the most handsome face she'd ever seen.

"Oh…I…I'm…" She sounded like such a ninny instead of a woman of thirty.

She lost herself in the sea of his clear blue eyes. The

theatre, her mother's cruel words, the constant stares, all faded away and settled into this one perfect moment. His warm hands penetrated through her satin dress, searing her skin and sent her heart thundering.

She tried to think of something intelligent—or at least somewhat witty—to say but she was not used to conversing with handsome men who disrupted her senses. "I…I apologize for ruining—"

"You didn't ruin anything," the handsome stranger's deep masculine voice quickly set her at ease. His fervent gaze stirred a long-forgotten flutter in her stomach.

She did not want the moment to end but did not want him to be caught with her either. She fought to control her swirling emotions. "I best be returning to my party."

"I suppose I should release you." It almost sounded like he didn't want to.

Her heart soared for a brief moment before reality pierced it with an arrow, sending it crashing to the ground. Although there was something familiar about him that she couldn't quite place, it was clear this gentleman was new to London, otherwise he would have already set her to her feet, bid adieu, and run the other way. The gossipmongers could be altogether too cruel to those who came near the Cursed Heiress.

"Yes, I suppose," she whispered. Despite the glorious feel of his warm hands holding her, it *was* for the best. Her life's path was clear, straight and narrow.

Although not quite ready to face her family, she slipped quietly into the box and took her seat, praying her mother might have some compassion for her frayed nerves.

"So, you've decided to return?" Mother's tone was hard and disapproving.

Sabina had hoped to have a pleasant visit with her brother, but current company made it impossible. Rigidly holding her tears in check, she tried to maintain her composure for peering eyes, tried to ignore her mother's slights and Eunice's harsh glare, tried to ignore the stares and hushed mockery from the gossipmongers, but she was only human.

Mustering whatever calmness still within her power, she politely excused herself. It was the one positive aspect to being a spinster—she could come and go as she pleased. No sooner had she retreated down the grand staircase than curious onlookers were weaving tales about the Cursed Heiress. She picked up her pace and never looked back.

ABOUT THE AUTHOR

Award winning historical romance author Alanna Lucas grew up in Southern California, but always dreamed of distant lands and bygone eras. From an early age, she took an interest in history and travel, and is thrilled to incorporate those diversions into her writing. Alanna writes Regency-set historical romance.

When she is not daydreaming of her next travel destination Alanna can be found researching, spending time with family, or going for long walks. She makes her home in California with her husband, children, one sweet dog, and hundreds of books.

Just for the record, you can never have too many shoes, handbags, or books. And travel is a must.

Find Alanna online at www.alannalucas.com

facebook.com/AuthorAlannaLucas

twitter.com/alannalucas27

bookbub.com/authors/alanna-lucas

ALSO BY ALANNA LUCAS

When the Marquess Returns

A Marquess in Waiting and the Cursed Heiress…

The *ton* is abuzz and mamas are lining up their daughters; identical twins Maximus and Lucius St. Albans are making their entry into society. But they're not just eligible—they're the missing grandsons of the Duke of Warrington, stolen as infants.

However, Maximus doesn't relish the battle with his cocky, reprobate brother to be the next Marquess. And he has no time for the simpering misses now vying for his attention. Only Miss Sabina Teverton has his interest.

She was resigned to life as a spinster but from the moment Sabina meets Lord Maximus, her heart is torn. She dreams of a match with him—but how can that be when she's been branded as cursed…and she knows secrets of that night long ago when Maximus and his twin were snatched from their cradles?

Only a Hero Will Do

Defender of the realm…and his wary heart…

Captain Grant Alexander is an enigma in London society. Dashing and handsome, he coldly eschews marriage. But the *ton* knows nothing of his role in the Legion: to bring Typhon, the traitor who seeks to destroy the British monarchy, to justice.

When Grant is thrown together with fellow Legion member Elizabeth Atwell, he's instantly beguiled yet exasperated by this beautiful viscount's daughter. She has little interest in combing the marriage mart for a well-bred, well-heeled husband, but is adept at code-breaking and handling a bow and arrow. She also refuses to do as she is told, insisting she accompany Grant on his mission.

As Typhon continues to evade capture and dark forces are at work, Grant realizes he must act, not only to protect the realm but Elizabeth too…not to mention his heart, which is in danger of thawing every time she comes close…

In His Arms Series:

Face to Face

When We Dance

Mistletoe Waltz

Dancing Around the Truth

Wish Upon a Waltz

Waltzing with the Earl

23615343R00066

Made in the USA
San Bernardino, CA
28 January 2019